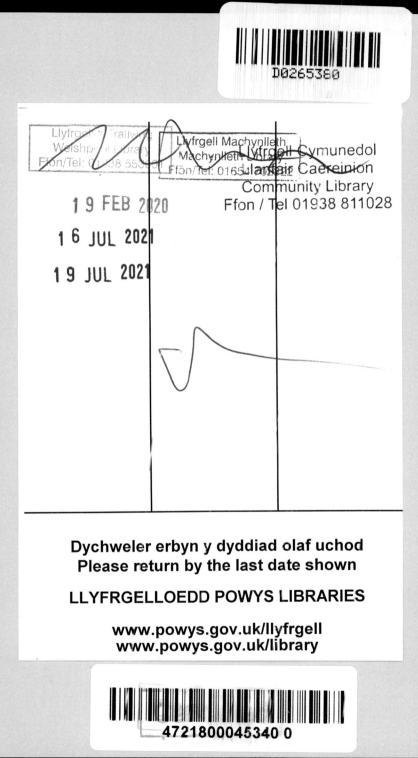

BRIEF LIVES

Also by Christopher Meredith

Novels
Shifts
Griffri
Sidereal Time
The Book of Idiots

Poetry
This
Snaring Heaven
The Meaning of Flight
Black Mountains
Air Histories
Still Air (with Sara Philpott)

For children
Nadolig bob Dydd
Christmas Every Day

As editor
Five Essays on Translation (with Katja Krebs)
Moment of Earth

Translation
Melog a novel by Mihangel Morgan

BRIEF LIVES

six fictions

Christopher Meredith

Seren is the book imprint of
Poetry Wales Press Ltd
57 Nolton Street, Bridgend, Wales, CF31 3AE
www.serenbooks.com
Facebook: facebook.com/SerenBooks
Twitter: @SerenBooks

ISBNs
Hardback – 978-1-78172-452-1
Ebook – 978-1-78172-465-1
Kindle – 978-1-78172-466-8

A CIP record for this title is available from the British Library.

The publisher acknowledges the financial assistance of the Welsh
Books Council.

Printed by TJ International, Cornwall.

Cover: © Tim Marshall, www.unsplash.com

ACKNOWLEDGEMENTS

Most of this work appears here for the first time but some pieces, sometimes in earlier versions, have appeared in *Best European Fiction 2015* (ed. West Camel), *Planet*, *The Interpreter's House*, *Anglo-Welsh Review*, *After the First Death* (ed. Tony Curtis) and *Dodos and Dragons* (eds A. Arjanee, M. Jenkins and K. Vadamootoo). 'Averted Vision' was broadcast on BBC Radio Wales in a version for two voices, produced by Ceri Meyrick.

Readers of my poetry will notice that the final story in this volume also appeared in my collection *Snaring Heaven*. I'm as certain as I've ever been of anything that it belongs in both books.

Several books have been called *Brief Lives* and I didn't mean to add to their number. But I've realised that the working title was working harder than I thought, so I've yielded to the need to be unoriginal this time, like those composers and visual artists who sometimes take their titles from the common store, partly in acknowledgement that we're all in this together.

My thanks to Penny Thomas for her help with this and other work, to Jeremy Hooker for his perceptive reading of some of the stories, and to Barry McAuley for his expert advice.

CONTENTS

AVERTED VISION

Edwards knew that he ought to be dead.

He was used to the smell and the sea was calmer. Calm sea and starfroth, the unfamiliar constellations. The spew-stench from the hold, but then just turn your head and there were lungfuls of pure air with salt for flavour, the dark sea broken with the glitter of points of starlight.

The day before he'd been sick when the underbalasted coalship had pitched in the huge swell.

Christ, he'd thought. This is the worst thing in the world. Worse than the dysentery. Then, shut up, you dull bugger – you're alive.

*

Lovat looked at the stars. He was used to the dark and could see the blue or red tinge of some of them, thought he could detect, here and there, the faint films of nebulae. He wished he knew more about it, thought he would have to get a book. But then, some luck and another month or so and they'd be home.

He hung his head back and stared straight up. The fixed stars shifted with the ship's movement. A point of light came into being as it crossed the edge of his field of view and then vanished when he tried to look straight at it. He looked slightly away again and it reappeared. Averted vision, that was called. Something to do with how the eye works in the dark. Look away slightly and faint objects get clearer. He remembered reading that.

He felt his tommy gun slide away on his knees and grabbed it with a start. He looked across the hatch, but Edwards had his face turned away, looking out to sea.

Lovat looked up once more.

*

Like them, Edwards thought. They all ought to be dead.

He didn't look down into the hold where his feet dangled above the sleeping prisoners.

They must think it too. Every day he thought, why am I still alive? In the hold beneath his swinging heels where there should have been thousands of tons of coal, the prisoners lying in one another's dried vomit must be glad to be alive. But they were only second line stuff, clerks and all. They were only moved in after the front line men had finished. So perhaps they didn't realise they all ought to be dead.

He looked at Lovat.

He didn't know he ought to be dead. Came too late.

Sorry, Private Lovat. We all know how much you wanted to do your bit and so on. But it finished ten minutes ago.

What a shame. But never mind. Help me to disinter the pieces of my former friends and give them Christian whatsits. The many men so beautiful. Fragments whirling in the void like stars. And help me, Lovat, on the fence at Sham Shui Po.

Show them who's boss and so on, the pillock of a subaltern says, *just till things calm down a bit*.

And do you love that, Lovat? Strutting with a gun?

Edwards realised he was gripping his machine gun very tight.

*

Stare straight up like this, straight at a faint object in gloom, and it vanishes. Huge catastrophes on the other side of space, tricked into oblivion by some technical hitch in the retina.

Staring at the invisible far sun, Lovat felt the tension draining from his limbs, his eyes getting heavy, seeming to drag down his face.

His father, waving the scissors, said, 'Keep your nose clean and your head down, and for them as sneers at your trade, tell em barbering's preferable to barbarity.'

He wiped the two sinks in front of the mirrors, checked the floor for yesterday's clippings.

'And don't tell your mother about the johnnies. It's a good sideline and comes natural with the trade. People often feel like a bit of the other after a trim and a nice bit of smelly stuff on the bonce. Frustrated conception's no sin. Frustrated people – now that is something that can end up messy.'

Handy to have a trade. In the army it'd come in useful, like playing the trumpet, they said. Help you avoid the bad bits. Ballocks. You end up cutting everybody's hair and loading the bodies onto the lorries, standing around by the fence with a gun, acting hard. The peaked cap studiously looking away after he tells you, in his indirect way, to do something nasty. Still, not long. This is a trade mission, sort of. Japs for coal. This is how civilisation reasserts itself. Clear up the bodies and screw the best deal you can out of em before they can have their young men back. Just hang on. Live through it and we may get back to our own side of the planet. Keep your head clean and your nose. No. That wasn't it.

*

Edwards watched Lovat, sitting with his feet dangling in the opposite corner of the hatch, fall asleep. There was little light, but he saw Lovat's head sink forward. The imitation of death. The many men so beautiful and they all dead did lie and a thousand thousand slimy things.

Edwards glanced away at the glittering on the black ocean. About and about in reel and rout. And when they reared the elfish light fell off in hoary flakes. How was it?

He couldn't see Lovat's eyes but knew the lids were rolling down, the pupils up. Ah, sleep it is a gentle thing beloved from pole to pole, so take your nightshift sentry go and stick it up your.

Something moved, sliding on Lovat's knees. A dull glimmer.

The tommy gun clanged on the steel ladder as it fell into the hold. It hit the rungs several times as it must have turned end over end.

Edwards was up and starting down the ladder when he heard a strangled shout.

He looked up and called, 'Lamp, wanker.'

Lovat's torch flickered over the edge of the hatch.

'Shit. It nearly went once before.'

'Down here quick before they twig.'

Edwards hung out on the ladder with one hand and held his gun in the other.

Somebody groaning. Lovat passed him, panting, the torch beam jiggling.

The thin ray moved over the still figures, picked out the promontories of hips and shoulders.

'No fucker woke.'

Edwards saw Lovat stoop, pick up the fallen machine gun, and look at the man who had his hands on his face. Lovat looked towards the ladder.

'Come and have a look at this, taff.'

*

Fucking cunt. What did you go and lie there for? Nobody wanted you in Singapore. Nobody wanted you under the bastard hatch. You taking up astronomy or something?

Lovat pulled the prisoner's hands away from his face.

The man was still conscious. One eye was closing with a swelling. The nose was spread across the other cheek and his upper lip had split in a very clean straight line. The front teeth were smashed and the man, looking frightened up at Lovat, gargled blood.

*

No fucker woke? You must be greener than I thought. Why couldn't you keep your arm through the bastard strap?

Edwards looked at the still forms as he came down the ladder and moved slowly towards Lovat.

That's right. Keep your heads down.

He glanced at the injured face in the pool of torchlight and looked round the hold once more. The smell of vomit and coal.

'Well done, Lovat.'

'He's only a jap.'

He's a jap, I'm a taff. Who the fuck are you?

'Well we can't leave him like that. He's being fucking repatriated day after tomorrow.'

'They aren't in a position to complain though, are they?'

Edwards looked round at Lovat whose face was dimly lit from below. A light to make faces demonic, but Lovat looked merely scared.

'Get the fucker up. See if he can walk and get him aft to be patched up.'

Lovat put the gun down, thought, picked the gun up and put the torch down and pulled at the prisoner's upper arm. The man got to his feet, a little unsteadily, holding his head back as if he was afraid part of his face might slide off. He was wearing only shorts. Edwards watched the torchlight jiggle as Lovat followed the man up the ladder.

Fucking marvellous. Leave me in the dark.

Edwards got up behind them quickly and went back to his place at the corner of the hatch.

Three hundred odd of them. The promontories of hips and shoulders. The path of weak light flickered in his mind.

For a charnel dungeon fitter. Why am I still?

*

Lovat pressed the muzzle of his gun into the man's back as they walked aft.

Just like the films, except he's very tall. Thin, from the camp of course. They were supposed to be little and yellow and wear thick glasses. They were inscrutable heathens.

He looked at the tall man's starved back. What muscle there was was sculpted by the upward angled torchbeam. The notched spine was clear.

They fuck up people like Edwards. Looks forty but he's twenty-five. Time I'm twenty-five all I want is to be a barber flogging rubber johnnies to customers wanting to enjoy what comes natural after a bit of preening. There's pleasure in that exactness. The precise clipping, the perfectly razored back of the neck, the carefully angled hand mirror allowing him to inspect your razorwork while you discuss the match. Stepping into the yard of an evening with a packet of Craven A, watching Orion or whatever arcing up over the shed. Keep your head down and your nose clean. Or keep your nose on your face, anyway.

Unpleasantly, Lovat felt himself smiling.

Clean. Was it worth getting the MO out of his bunk? The peaked cap giving me long hard look. How? Do you really expect me to believe? Seen your sort. Quiet and then they get a taste for it. Really, now it's all finished too. You'd change your tune if you'd seen half the.

Edwards was half way round the bend. Stuttered and said he'd been six stone when they took him out of it before his last leave. They did that. Peaked caps and heathens. And who would count them the other end? Who counted?

Lovat glanced back. They were passing between the rail and some superstructure. Edwards was no longer in sight.

Lovat whispered, 'Stop.'

He moved inboard of the prisoner and nudged his shoulder with the muzzle so that they faced one another, Lovat with his back to the bulkhead, the man with his back to the sea, pushed back against the rail. In the upturned beam Lovat saw that the bruises had ripened. Blood still streamed from his nose and mouth. The closed eye was buried in a fold of swellings. The unharmed eye looked startlingly ordinary, a dark brown, the tiny map of blood vessels in the white. Almost, Lovat thought, intelligent. Almost, even, real.

Staring straight at the man's face, Lovat snapped the torch off. He continued staring but the face had disappeared.

*

Edwards knew how it would be. Lovat would come back. Edwards would say, That was quick. Lovat would be quiet a moment and then say. Edwards would say nothing. Lovat would say why. Try to. And that would be all.

Edwards held his gun loosely across his lap. A tenseness passed through him as if he would vomit and he unclipped the magazine, threw it to one side. He relaxed.

The torchlight danced on the deck towards him, flickered momentarily across one pair of walking feet.

Above the far thrumming of the engines and the purling of water around the hull, Edwards had heard nothing.

PROGRESS

On a spring day in the middle of the twentieth century a thin young man got off the half past ten bus to Glynderi and stood at the end of the long concrete footbridge. There were no shops and few houses just here and the road was deserted. The young man had no cap and as it was mild he wore his raincoat unbuckled and unbuttoned.

It had felt a bit awkward on the bus, with only a few women on board. saying nothing, their heads swaying in time with the rocking of the journey. Since he had left the house – the rooms – that morning, he had said four words, and they were: Return to Glynderi, please. The conductor, with his scratched leather money pouch, had said nothing either as he wrote the ticket, lounging against the end of a chrome backrest with casual professionalism. The young man had felt them all, you know, looking at him without looking, assuming that to be on a bus at this time on a week-day he must have no job.

But he had taken a day off without pay, and could have come down on the train for nothing, being a railwayman. It was just that he did not want anybody at the station to know that he was looking for something that paid better. What was it to them? The rent took a lot, and the baby was not really a baby any more. We could do with a bit more, his wife had said.

So now he had his feet on this bridge again for the first time in eight, nine years. He could see nobody. It was the middle of a shift and it was quiet at first, but a little after the bus had gone he started to hear, faintly, the throbbing and wheezing of the compressors drawing new air down. Occasional clangs and calls came from the yard hidden by the buildings beyond the far end of the bridge. Just under its surface the day was filled with muted percussions and detonations.

He breathed in through his nose and felt for the cigarettes in his pocket. There were three Woodbines left in the packet of ten. He took one out. Open raincoat, Brylcreemed hair. Their casualness was counterpointed by the Windsor knot in his tie. But there was no one here to see him. The yard buildings where the clangs came from were closed on themselves, turned away from him and from the arch of the mountain beyond, blank. The retort shapes of the three scaffolds seemed to be looking past one another and into the distance, somewhere else.

Once, when he had worked here, in the search before the shift, they had found a dogend in his pocket. The skewed last half an inch of a cigarette he had forgotten about and not even a match to light it, but they had still fined him.

He put the cigarette in his mouth and felt in the other pocket for the matches.

Three quid. More than a week's pay. It was supposed to be about safety, but it was a racket. Or it had been then. Because things were better now, weren't they? It was all different. Things had happened. There were new managers and new owners. There had been events. Events.

He rattled the matchbox and walked a few paces onto the bridge. Then slowed and stopped. Because on bridges, on foot, there is always the tug of that need to pause mid way. That was it. The need to stop and look over whatever it was that you were intersecting. To look and to become, for anybody looking up at you, a punctuation mark.

Just then a man stepped onto the other end of the bridge, walking towards him. He was small and wore a cap and mackintosh and carried a wood block under his arm. As he drew near he gave a sideways look that seemed selfconscious, and a minimal nod. His face was not properly washed and his eyelashes were still crusted with black. The hand not doubled under the block was heavily bandaged and held stiffly in front of him like some grotesque trophy. His mouth opened a fraction and perhaps, as he passed, he murmured, Aye-aye, or perhaps he did not.

The thin young man almost nodded as he turned away to lean on the crumbling parapet. Taking a match from the box, he glanced at the collier's retreating back. He could have asked if there was any danger of work there, something like that. There were stock responses of the stock cynicism that the other man could have made. But the collier was in no mood to pause. He had got off early because he had had a smack. You could not wash as you should with your hand bandaged like that.

Underneath the bridge, instead of a river, there were the railway lines on different levels, the standing coal wagons, filled and waiting. They were not even hopper wagons. That had not changed. They had used the same rolling stock for thirty years. His age. If you looked straight down, straight down, and blinkered out the pale spring greens of the banks of the valley right at the edges of vision, there was no colour there at all.

In his first week, sixteen years before, helping to put a prop in, he had lost three fingernails. In the monochrome lamplight and the fuzz of dust there had been the sudden gash of opened flesh and lipstick blood, the colour of Claudette Colbert's mouth on a cinema poster. Good god, butty, his butty had said, you'll soon run out of fingers like that. The nails grew back of course.

He lit the cigarette and dropping the box back into his pocket, flicked the spent match out into the motionless black river. A brief tracer of smoke followed it.

The wagons were packed with the huge chunks of steam coal. Their complications and the patterning of latches and buffers, the hatchwork of sleepers choked the eyes with their detail. And nobody was down there to observe him, a piece of dark toothed out against the sky, to read what he might mean. Everybody was elsewhere, at work. A few hundred paces away, over the bridge, in the yard stacked with Doughty arches, near the lamp room, was an office, and in it by a stove, perhaps today unlit, some man sat at a desk.

The young man would give his name there, announce a meaning for himself and see a ledger open, join some list, or perhaps even walk into a job. He would do that.

The smoke had filled him, answering a small craving.

But he liked the railways. It gave him unreasoning pleasure to pin and unpin the brakes from Dowlais Top to Quaker's Yard. Even to latch and unlatch wagons in icy sidings on bonefreezing mornings was vital, somehow. To be involved in the flowing of people over the earth in the ordinary processes of life.

He extended his palms to blot out the black tangle of the dead river and looked, calmly, at the backs of his hands.

You had to weigh that against the three rented rooms, the infestation of black pats, the cockroaches with nowhere to go at the cold end of the terrace. Corned beef and potatoes. They could, she was right. They could do with a bit more.

But there were the events, the changes.

Under his nose the end of the cigarette flared in needlepoints of heat.

You could, so to speak, dig back down through them. For a decade and a half events had fallen like annihilating snow.

And indeed there had been the worst winter anybody could remember. His father, after fifty odd years working in a place like this, had retired. Was the end of something an event? Surely yes. He had become a father himself. The baby, who was not a baby any more, had been born in a hospital. A real hospital. There had been a significant election.

He had travelled. In Madras he had sat next to a young Englishwoman at a concert and talked with her of politics. He had played cards with Lascars on the deck of a ship. He had had dysentery. He had stood on islands on the other side of the world. He had married. There had been the tribunal at which he had argued his way out of a reserved occupation. There had been alliances, declarations and so on. He had followed history's argument in those years. And so right back under the drift to the boy not long out of school crouching in the dark with a bloodied hand.

And he had, somewhere in the middle of all this, between talking to the English lady about the meaning of Gandhi and becoming a father and a railway guard, somewhere there, he had killed a lot of people.

Yes. That had happened too.

The snow cleared from before him. He could see his left hand thrust forward over the parapet, the fingers curled as if holding something angled straight ahead. His right hand, in a similar attitude, was almost under his chin.

Out of the silence the throbbing of the compressors came back. There was a percussion of buffers and a dull rolling as the complicated black river started to move under him.

His shoulders, arms, and fingers unseized. He placed his hands, calmly, before himself again. They shook a little, as usual at these times. He watched the mechanical unlocking and articulating of the fingers. When he took the cigarette from his mouth the end of it was a crimped and wetted oval.

These summaries both shook and soothed him. They assured him that, yes, something had happened after all. They could tell you, somehow, what you meant. It was meant to be better. His grandfather had gone down when he was eight, his father at eleven, and he at fourteen. That was progress. Little Cary had been born in a ward, with electricity and hot water and oxygen.

But this. He glanced at the scaffolds. Three thieves. They were unchanged dead towers. They unsaid the drift of things.

He tapped the long finger of ash from his cigarette onto the wagons below. The old owners' names were still painted in smirched white on their sides.

It might be the same people, on the gate, in the office, nine years fatter. That would rub your nose in it. And he could smell, taste the place. Diesel and grease. Whitewash. Horses. The burning cud of twist. Carbolic. Stale urine. The zinc rim of the water-jack against the teeth. You could turn up quietly and take all that and if you were lucky, occasionally you might sneak back early to the land of the living, with your hand in a dirty bandage and a shifty look in your eye.

No. He said the word out loud to the wagons.

This was how it would be. He would tell her how he had talked to the spotter on the gate. How he had walked into the yard. There were the steel arches stacked in the same place after all these years. In the office by the lamp room the stove was unlit. The man there was decent enough but did not even bother looking in the ledger. No, he had said. There was nothing. On the way back he talked to somebody he knew on the weighbridge and got the same story.

He would tell her this, and never in the rest of their lives would he tell her how, on the middle of the bridge, he pinched the fire from his cigarette, dropped the unsmoked portion of it in his pocket, and turned back.

THE CAVALRY

Later that Christmas morning she got the two boys ready.

'We're gwnna see Bert' she said, 'it en far' and she was surprised they didn' complain.

But then, they'd been up before six and unwrapping presents and playing ever since. They'd had the first burst of excitement with the stocking presents on their beds and then rushed down to the presents on the armchairs in front of the fire in the best room. Dil had lit the fire at about half past four before he went to work, before she got up herself. She put some coal on both fires now. It was scarcely cold at all outside, but the presents room was always chilly, except for these twelve days of the year. The chicken was in the oven on low and it'd be okay till they came back. The boys could keep their uniforms on over their ordinary clothes. They didn' need coats in this. She put some bits and pieces in her shopping bag.

Mark had been going between his annuals and his drawing book and the plastic soldiers. They were green and little, moulded on rectangular bases in one piece. They were shiny and unpainted and you could see thin seams of plastic sticking up in places. He held them close and looked hard to see their faces. They had noses, and hollows for eyes, and mouths, but it was difficult to see much. Sometimes he put them along the tiles by the fire and the flickering flames shone on the plastic. It was a small fireplace, not so hot as the one in the living room, and all year it was empty and cold like a dark open mouth, except for now. Now it was alive with colours and warmth. Sometimes he put the soldiers by the tree lights. They'd never had tree lights before. They had small pointy tinted bulbs and small transparent tinted plastic collars, fretted like petals. His father had fixed the last, yellow, light almost at the top of the tree, by the cardboard fairy Mark had had to make in school again that year. He'd tried to make it more interesting this time but it still wasn' very good. He'd drawn an open mouth as if the fairy was talking or singing. The other lights wound down through the branches on their thin green cable. They spread the warm light in patterns on the green needles and the hanging decorations and across the small table the tree stood on, where he positioned some of the soldiers. There were soldiers with rifles and soldiers with machine guns and some with their arms spread out throwing grenades, and two with radios, and one had a big gun with a tube on it leading to a pack on his back. But the faces and the seams and the light were more interesting.

Lee was quiet, sitting eating sweets on the floor by his armchair, his plastic silver gun in its holster.

In the kitchen she checked the flame in the gas oven and made sure the oven door was shut tight, and she stepped into the room with the boys and switched the main light off, but she left the tree lights on.

When the big light went off Mark liked how the fire and the tree lights got brighter and shone more on the tiles and the soldiers and shone on the laminated covers of the annuals on the floor. On one cover Korky the Cat had a huge face. He was smiling and his eyes looked strange, big like that, with long green slits in them. It was better inside the annual, where the coloured pictures were alive in their boxes, the size they ought to be.

In the other annual every so often there was a page called Amazing Facts! Unbelievable But True! He had been through the annual looking for these. Sometimes there were four or five Amazing Facts! on the same page in little sections.

One was about How Animals See! Bees can see colours we can't and horses have eyes that magnify things and eagles have such sharp eyesight they could read a newspaper from hundreds of yards away, only they'd have to learn to read first. Another was about The Great Houdini's Escapes! The one he liked best was Alexander Selkirk: The Real Robinson Crusoe! Mr Davies in school had read to them about Robinson Crusoe. Alexander Selkirk lived on a desert island too, but he wasn' like Robinson Crusoe because Robinson Crusoe was shipwrecked but Alexander Selkirk asked to be put ashore because the ship was dangerous, but after they went he was sorry. He was *marooned*. They were always looking for treasure, gold and silver, pieces of eight, in those days but there wasn' much about treasure in Alexander Selkirk's story. On the Amazing Facts! page there was a drawing done with a black pen of Robinson Crusoe with his fur hat and beard, sitting in his cave with a parrot on a perch to talk to, and then a picture of Alexander Selkirk with clothes made of animal skins running after a goat. He learned to outrun a goat! it said. Once a ship came and he thought he was rescued, but it was the Enemy and he had to hide up a tree a long time. When he was really rescued years later he could barely talk and they couldn' understand him at first.

She got the boys into the kitchen and pulled little Lee into shape. He was singing to himself and playing with the holster as she tugged the uniform straight and got his shoes on. He was already wearing the hat.

Mark closed the door slowly on the magic room and its tree lights and the firelight. The room would stay like this. The new coal would burn a bit brighter, but everything else would just wait for them.

Lee turned his eyes to look up at Mark while his shoelaces were being tied. 'Hey' he said. 'Did you know already? We're going to see old Burp.'

'Bert' Mark said.

Sometimes she talked about Bert and the others to their father. About little Philly, and Mrs Lane, and Matty Griffiths, the old people she went to on the Home Help. Little Philly just sat by the fire all day. Mrs Lane said funny words that made her laugh. She said consternated instead of constipated. Matty Griffiths never went upstairs. All she said about Bert was: Poor old bugger.

*

Christmas didn' happen outside the house like you thought it would. It was grey and grainy and unmoving and nobody was about. It was like the day went on being itself, as if it didn' care what it was supposed to be like.

The cloud was down on the ridges of the hills like a lid. You felt like you could almost touch it. Mark wanted to stretch up and try but he didn't because he knew he couldn' really. He looked back at the houses to see if the cloud was brushing the chimneys but it wasn't. Sometimes it did.

They crossed the road and went downhill across the bit of grass and through the streets of the estate. The houses were all quiet and there were no cars and you couldn' see anybody. They went down the big curving hill towards the town. It was very steep. If you were on a horse it would lean back so it didn' slide. Mark leaned back and clucked his tongue to the horse.

She felt Lee dragging on her arm as she held his hand, acting tired.

'Come on, Dai' she said. 'It en far now. You're getting too big to carry all the way.'

'Dwn call him Dai' Mark said.

'Quite right' she said. 'I shouldn' call him Dai. En it, Dai?'

Mark carried her shopping bag to help. He held it in front of him with both hands gripping the handles, like they were reins.

They came to the end of the council houses and to the start of the terrace. The last estate house had the gable end of the terrace instead of one of its front garden walls. She'd known it before the estate was built but it was hard to remember. The terrace of Stanley Street used to point up the hill to nothing but open mountain and a coal tip, some old farm. Yet it wasn' all that long ago. When Mark was just toddling. Not that long after the first baby.

She felt a tightening inside her, a dead chill. She pushed the memory away.

She squeezed Lee's hand. It was warm and he wiggled his fingers and swung her arm and skipped a step or two. The tightening unravelled itself.

It was still unchristmassy here. Mark looked at the front room windows as they passed. It must be funny to have no front garden. If there were people in all these houses, you couldn' tell. Perhaps it was like this all the way down into town and round the town clock. Everywhere deserted, and only them and Bert left. There were Christmas lights round the clock but they were just like ordinary bulbs really, only coloured, not like the tiny pointy bulbs on the tree.

She knocked Bert's door. The boys looked up at the house. Bert's was one of the ones that had cement stuck over the stonework. It was grey and streaked.

Mark looked at the front room window next to the door. The curtains were drawn shut but the wire at the top was sagging and they parted from one another in a long thin triangle. It was too dark to see through the gap. The curtains were dirty. Inside the window on the wide sill among some dead flies was a big ornamental figure of a little girl. It was so big it was the size of a real baby. It was painted orangey and yellowy colours and it wasn' very shiny. She had fat legs that were moulded together and sandals and she had a hat that was meant to be a sort of straw hat. Her face was in a dead sort of smile and her eyes were dull. She was grubby and chipped, and there were chunks knocked off her nose and one cheek and the brim of her hat where you could see the bright white chalky stuff she was made of.

As the door opened slowly and a white face came from the dark, Lee's hand tightened on his mother's.

'Merry Christmas, Bert' she said.

Bert's face showed no sign of surprise but out of his already open mouth came a semi-coherent 'Good god.'

'On'y a flying visit. I brought the boys if tha's all right. I couldn' leave em.'

'Well well' Bert said.

'This is my big boy, Mark, and this is my other big boy, Lee.'

Only his eyes moved down to Mark and Lee and he slowly turned away and walked up the passage. She got the boys up the high step and they followed him, having to go slow. Mark watched Bert's back going slowly into the dark. He was wearing a grey coat and a flat cap like Mark's dad said he would never wear. They passed the closed door of the room

39

where the chipped girl stood trapped behind the curtains on the high sill, and they turned into another dark room at the back of the house.

There was a table in the middle with not much on it. There was a black fireplace like in their uncle's house, only in this one, behind the bars, there was almost no fire. It was ashy white and low and there was little warmth. In a corner an opening led into another small room. A narrow window onto the back yard was the only light. On the dark wall where the fireplace was a few pictures were hanging. There was a smell of cat.

Instead of turning his neck, Bert turned his whole body when he wanted to look round. He held his shoulders forward like he couldn' stand up straight and all his movements were slow and small. You could hear him breathing.

He sat down in a ruined armchair by the low fire.

'Well well' he said again.

His mouth didn' move much when he spoke. Mark heard a muffled voice from far down in the throat, as if somebody in a cave was calling to people outside.

'Home Help on Christmas day. Well well.'

'Best time, mun' she said. She took the bag from Mark and put it on the table but she didn' get anything out. 'You got to show willing.'

Bert leaned forward and pushed on the armrests. 'Tea.'

'Stay put' she said. 'I'll put the kettle on.' She went through the corner door to the scullery, getting her matches out, and he leant back. She came back in and knelt by the fire. 'I'll put a bit on this, Bert, and some slack on the top.' She laid some bigger lumps first then shovelled on some smaller coal from the bucket. It wasn' cold but it'd keep in for later. She took the grimy dust pan and brush off their hooks on the companion set and swept round the hearth, and then the coconut mat in front of it and threw the dust on the fire. Mark watched how firmly and certainly she moved. The bristles on the brush were almost worn away as if it was a hundred years old.

She moved around tidying things here and there. She took the opened tin of cat food with a fork stuck in it from the table and put it in the scullery. When she came back in she saw that Lee had slackened his grip on Mark's hand, which he'd taken when they came in to the house, and the boys were looking round, not moving from the patch of floor they'd been led to.

Bert said something she didn' understand.

'Wha' d'ou say, Bert?'

Mark listened hard as Bert tried again.

'Where's your Home Help coat?'

She had a blue nylon coat for work with buttons up the front and letters stitched in a circle on the pocket like a badge saying Home Help Service. It was a bit big for her. It looked new.

'I en working today, mun' she said.

'You are then.' He looked at Mark as if he was sharing

some joke and made a brief low noise that might have been a laugh. 'Coming to see me. Well well. Haven' seen you without your Home Help coat before.'

She was getting the few things out of the bag and putting them on the table. Mark and Lee watched in case there was something for them.

'Now, I can't stay long. We got the dinner in and these boys have got things to do.'

'Where's Dil?'

'Working days today. And tomorrow.'

'Well well. All work.'

Lee's voice came high and clear after the muffled cave voice: 'They do keep the cookers lit.'

She paused with a packet in her hand and looked at her younger son. 'Tha's right, Dai' she said. 'Good boy. He do listen to his father see, Bert. He mean the Coke Ovens. Somebody got to do it.'

'The Plant never sleeps' Mark said, and then he felt stupid for speaking.

'He wn be home till gone half past three' she said. 'No service bus today see. Now listen.'

She sounded like she was giving a warning but really it was her friend voice.

'There's a bit of plain cake for you. Not much mind. And two slices of ham. On'y little bits.' She wagged two grease-proof packets and put them down. 'And dwn give em to the bloody cat. You got to eat. And here's your card.'

Mark had seen her writing quickly on the Christmas card that morning. It had a snowy town on it with a horse and carriage and people in top hats and red bonnets, and the snow was piled on the frames of bright yellow windows. There was an oldfashioned lamp with yellowy light and there was a bit of glitter round a spire near the top of the picture that was meant to be snowflakes.

'And here you are, you bugger.' She pulled out a packet of cigarettes. 'Players Weights. Tha's the ones en it?'

Bert tried to turn his head to look but couldn' get far. He pushed himself up from the chair and turned his body and stepped to the table and he looked at the presents but didn' touch them, not even the envelope.

'Well well. Thank you.'

'Want one now?'

'No thank you.'

She watched his hands hesitating in the gloom near the table's edge.

'The fire've brightened up a bit' she said. 'Why you in the dark, mun, Bert?'

The kettle whistled and she went into the scullery to make the tea. After she'd put the water on the pot she looked round. There were some dried corned beef sandwiches between two plates on the draining board. The top plate was nudged to one side and the cat had been nibbling a corner. She cut off the chewed portion and threw it out the back door. She got the brush and gave the scullery lino a sweep, brushing the dust out the back too. The threshold bar was missing. He used an old towel along the floor to keep the draught out.

Bert looked at the two boys and his mouth move a little in the direction of a smile. There was a tiny shake of his head. He took out a box of matches and reached above the table. Mark saw for the first time that there was a gaslight there. A pipe came out of the ceiling and there was a thin metal crossbar on it at an angle like a seesaw. Little rings hung from the ends of this seesaw on blackened chains. Bert struck a match and slowly drew down the upper arm of the seesaw by pulling the ring. There was a faint hissing till the mantle lit with a soft pop. It was rounded like a sort of acorn and it glowed bright white. You could see the tiny mesh it was made of like bandage getting whiter and whiter. And Bert's face was white too and covered in little cracks and dusty looking, except for a thin pink rim at the bottom of each eye. He didn' have any eyelashes. The pink disappeared when he looked down and the shadow of the cap slid over his face.

Mark had seen gaslights in a caravan in Porthcawl in the summer. They were on the walls of the caravan and pointed up and had glass covers. His father showed him how they worked and told him the word *mantle*. It could mean a cloak or a cover too. It was like *mantelpiece* as well. He told him how a long time ago, before even he was born, people used to light the gas coming straight out of the pipe, like on a cooker, but the light wasn' very strong. 'More heat than light' his father said. So they invented the mantle. It worked better because of *incandescence*. The tiny wire inside a lightbulb, the *element*, he said, did the same thing only better. In his father's house when he was a boy they didn' even have gas. They had an oil lamp and candles. And then later they went straight to lectric, but that wasn' till After the War.

The white mantle over the table had grown so intense you couldn' look at it. The light wasn' yellow. It was white like chalk. But somehow the edges of the room seemed just as dark.

His mother was putting a metal teapot on the table and then two cups and saucers.

'Thank you, Bert' she said. Tha's better, mun.'

He gestured at the boys with a stiff hand. 'What they wearing?'

She poured the tea and looked at them. The light was strong on the shiny nylon of their uniforms. Lee's big eyes were fixed on Bert. He had a serious expression. His silver gun was in his hand which was clamped to the top of his hat. Mark was standing very still and looking at the table.

'Coybows' Lee said, clearly. 'Coybow suits.'

Mark gave a sigh and whispered, '*Cowboy*.' Then 'Cavalry suits.'

'Cavalry uniforms, Bert' she said. 'There's good en it? They're the US Cavalry, see.' Then louder, 'US Cavalry.'

'Colonel Custard' Lee said.

Mark sighed.

'Well well.'

Bert moved back from the table and Mark could see his face again. He was trying to smile and his eyes looked a bit brighter and he was looking at him and Lee and making some noises but you couldn' quite understand.

Suddenly Mark knew that the uniform was stupid. Under the white glare the blue stuff it was made of looked thin and slippery. Mark's was tight round his middle and he'd had to squeeze it on over his jersey, and Lee's was big and loose on him. Mark liked the yellow stripe down the trouserleg and the yellow neckerchief, and the white cuff things were good but the rest was bad. The bits of black plastic that went round your ankle with a flap over your foot were useless. They were meant to be boots but they were silly. Lee had the good hat with a brim all the way round, a cowboy hat. Mark had wanted that, but he got the one with a peak at the front and a tipped-forward crown. It was a bit ugly, like Bert's cap. In the picture on the card that came with the packet that the uniform was in, the cavalryman had a big moustache and he looked stern, and the blue of the uniform was gentler. He was holding his rifle across his chest and smoke was swirling from the barrel and round the edge of the picture like a frame. Mark lowered his head and rubbed his hand where the nylon was tight on his belly.

She watched Mark looking down shyly with his hand on his tummy.

'Mark' she said, 'Bert is asking if you do like horses.'

'Gee gees' Bert said. 'See.' He walked to the wall where the fireplace was and half lifted a hand towards one of the pictures hanging there. 'See. That's me. I used to like the gee gees. Never made me rich mind.'

'Were you a coybow then?' Lee said.

Lee followed him, his hand still on his head, and uncertainly Mark went after.

Bert didn' say *gee gees* like it was baby talk, or Mark didn' think he did. The voice in the cave was too far away to know for sure. Perhaps it was because Bert's face was sort of frozen. But it sounded like he would have said *gee gees* even to another grownup.

The photograph wasn' one of those brownish ones like the one of Mark when he was a baby sitting on a carved chair with a fake background and very still. This one was a *snap*, only quite big, on hard shiny paper, very white and very black. There was a racehorse in the middle and other racehorses behind, but not running, just looking as if they were wandering around. People were walking among them. There was a jockey on the horse but it wasn' Bert. The jockey's leg was tucked up strangely on the saddle and he had a shiny boot and a peaked cap pushed back. He was small and spidery and sort of folded up. What was strangest about the horse was how big it was. It was immense. The muscle of its backside was black and tensed and shiny. One of the hooves was blurred a bit, and there were other little blurs here and there where the camera wasn' quick enough to

47

catch the movements. They were all over the picture but you had to look hard to find them. A man's trouserleg flapping as he walked, the tips of another man's fingers as he waved some signal. And the jockey's face too was blurred a little, as he was in the middle of turning and looking down as he went past. His eyes were just dark trails. He was looking down at Bert, who was standing at the side of the horse. But Bert wasn' looking at him. Bert was in the middle of the picture and didn' look much less old than he looked now. He was wearing a white coat like a doctor and a black bowler hat. The only time you saw bowler hats was in pictures or on the telly. Bert was a lot bigger than the jockey but the jockey was high above him on the gigantic horse. It was like nothing was in proportion. Bert was standing still, as he stood now, with his shoulders hunched a bit and his arms hanging at his sides, the palms of his hands turned to face back, his head stuck forward, and his mouth open a little. He wasn' looking at anything in particular. And here was the strange thing. The reason he looked so still was partly his way of standing, but also because not a bit of him was blurred. It was like he was the only still thing and all the rest of the world was swimming and changing. It was almost like his picture had been cut out and stuck on, but it hadn't.

'Aye. Gee gees all my life. That was me.' His breath wheezed out of the cave after the far voice stopped.

Lee was still staring at Bert's face. 'Are you gwnna die?' he said.

Mark winced and felt himself shrink, like slugs do with salt on them.

'Lee!' She paused, carrying the teacup from the table. 'You musn' say that, mun. Sorry, Bert. He's on'y little. We'll have a quick cup of tea and we'll have to go.' And to Lee, 'Watch it now, Dai.'

Mark watched Bert. Bert looked at Lee and his eyes moved to look at their mother, but not far enough. He turned his body a bit but still not enough. Instead he caught Mark's eye and a pink rim flickered as if he might be trying to wink. His eyes were bright like they'd been when he heard the word 'cavalry', and his stony face moved as if it would smile, but it couldn' get there.

From far down the words came to answer Lee: 'Like as not.'

He backed slowly to the armchair and sat down.

Mark unshrivelled a bit.

She gave Bert his tea and sat at the table. There was only the one armchair. 'Have some cake with it' she said.

'No thank you. Not just now.'

'Well dwn give it to the bloody cat then.'

Lee gathered close to her and Mark shuffled closer to her too and the boys waited till it was time to go.

The last thing Mark saw when they were leaving as she closed the door on the blackened kitchen was Bert reaching stiffly up over the table and tugging at the upper ring of the little seesaw to turn off the gaslight.

*

That evening Mark played in the room where his presents were. Lee was in the living room with their mother and father and the telly. Lee was still in his uniform, with the hat on. Mark had taken his off as soon as they got home. It was on the armchair with his other presents now, the hat on the armrest.

He lay on the floor with one of his annuals open. After a bit he turned the big light off. It made it too dark to read much, but the fire made light that flickered and slid. The tree lights tinged the pine needles and the tree decorations with different colours and the fretted plastic collars made their patterns. He put one plastic soldier on the soil round the tree in its pot, as if he was on a desert island, only up a cliff. Maybe he could escape or some of the others could rescue him later. It was the soldier with the strange gun with a tube coming from it.

Mark pretended to doze over his book. He was out in the hills of the island, under the pine trees, by a camp fire at night. Tomorrow him and his horse would look for the treasure. His horse was tied to a tree. It would be a brown horse, not black, with a white blaze on its face, and it wouldn' be as big as the horse in the photo.

After a bit the door cracked open and his father looked in. Mark thought he was going to say bedtime, because it felt late, but he didn't. He asked what he was doing and Mark

said Playing and he said In the dark? and Mark said Yes.
Then he said did he want to come and watch the film?

It was a shame to leave the fire and the lights on their own,
but nice to think of them too, still lighting the quiet room
and waiting for him. And anyway they'd stay up later if they
watched the film.

Mark's father clicked the light on and looked round the
room. He'd scarcely seen it since he lit the fire at half past
four. That could be left to burn down now. His son was
blinking in the light. It was a shame to break the subtle gauze
of dim light that Mark had settled in – the fire and the tiny
threads of electricity pouring into the new lights on the tree.
He reached up and touched the yellow bulb he'd fastened to
the topmost twig in front of Mark's cardboard angel. Almost
no heat. It was marvellous. Power from a coal furnace poured
down great cables and then it was refined down to this faint
whisper of energy, doing what you wanted it to, lighting up
the white face of a cardboard angel with wool hair and an open
mouth as if it was speaking. Making his Announcement.

'Your angel's just the job' he said.

Mark sighed. ''S a fairy. I do hate doing them.'

'I like the way you've done the mouth. I think he's saying
"Christmas is coming".'

He dropped his hand a bit awkwardly and looked at the
two chairs with their toys on them, Lee's a muddle of loud
colour and Mark's more organised, with boxes and books
stacked according to size, the toy uniform a ruffle of blue.

He saw she'd tidied up the wrapping paper. There wasn' anything needed doing. He'd managed an hour's sleep when he got home and had some dinner. He'd been done in but now he was revived a bit. It was nine and he was up early again tomorrow. Be better if he was tired and could sleep. He saw Mark's soldiers were in carefully angled positions on the low mantelpiece and on the hearth tiles.

'Move your men from by the fire, there's a good boy. You dwn wan' em to melt. I'll have to move em to do the fire in the morning anyway.'

Mark picked them up one by one and stood them on the arm of his chair in a row, opposite the cavalry cap.

His father's eye was led back to the tree on its small table next to the chair, and he noticed the lone figure standing on the earth in the bucket.

Mark watched his father as he lifted the figure between finger and thumb as if it was alive. The fingers twitched a bit at first as he examined the man. His face was expressionless as he rolled the soldier over in his palm.

'God' his father said. 'A flamethrower.'

'Is i'?' Mark took the figure from his hand and stared at it himself. His mother had a gas poker to light the fire. That had a tube coming out the back and little flames came out of holes in a flattened pipe, but she never used it. It wasn' safe, she said.

He pointed the flamethrower at the other men on the armrest and made a wooshing noise.

'Don't' his father said. 'Come on, Master, let's watch the film. It's a silent.'

Mark put the soldier back on his high desert island.

'A silent?' he said as they were going out. 'A whole long film of it?'

There was a programme on television on Sundays called Silents, Please! that showed bits from old silent films. A man talked about them and there was good music that changed with the mood of the films. They were a bit jerky and blurred sometimes and the people had staring white faces that often looked funny when they were meant to be scary and scary when they were meant to be funny. You couldn' always tell what they were meant to be. His father could remember the silents from when he was little but his mother couldn't really because his father was Just a Few Years Older. It was all Before the War.

His father switched the light off.

*

The living room wasn' as good as the presents room but it was warmer. Lee and his mother were on the settee. His father sat in an armchair and lit a cigarette. Mark lay on the mat with his feet pointing towards the television. The lamp with the yellow shade on top of the telly gave yellow light, and white light came from the telly and orange light came from the fire.

In Silents, Please! writing sometimes came on the screen to tell you a bit of what the jerky faces were saying. Sometimes the writing was on too long, but usually it was too quick for Mark. There'd be curly patterns on it sometimes and the shapes of the letters would be interesting, so that took his attention and he couldn' do the reading. His father told him that when he was a boy, in the pictures when the caption cards came up you could hear some people reading the words out to older people who couldn' read.

The announcer announced the film as if it was the most special thing there'd ever been on television. It was Charlie Chaplin's The Gold Rush.

Charlie Chaplin came on Silents, Please! sometimes but he wasn' as good as the other bits. Billy Bevan and Ben Turpin were funny and William S. Hart the cowboy was good. He had an oldfashioned hat with a big baggy top and baggy trousers that looked stupid and he looked quite old with a stony face, like Bert, but he was still good. When they fired the guns big puffs of smoke came out because there was no sound. And there was Fatty Arbuckle too. His mother said Matty Griffiths was like Fatty Arbuckle.

She felt Lee leaning against her, sleepy on the settee. Funny how somebody so little could make himself weigh so much. A dead weight. No. Not that. A live weight really. She knew about dead weights. He fidgeted now and then almost like he was still inside her. He was trying to keep his hat on even though it was buckled against her. Soon it'd be as shapeless as the old one she'd managed to prise off him on Christmas Eve.

On the screen a line of men were toiling over snowy mountains to get to the gold fields.

Lee had played and played but she'd managed to get some dinner down him. She thought of Bert, the dried sandwiches. She sucked on her cigarette.

'I should a took Bert a bit o dinner' she said. 'Plain cake and a slice o ham. What was I bloody thinking of.'

Dil watched the pale light of the television that poured over the floor and over Mark, lying on his back, dead straight, his hands under his head. He looked rigid and uncomfortable.

When Mark was a baby, in the rooms they'd rented – it must have been his first Christmas – they'd had a big tree he'd got from the new plantation after dark. And her nerves were still bad after the first baby even then, all that bloody mess. So he did some of the shopping and he saw the little candles and holders in Woolworth's made to go on the Christmas tree and he bought them and fixed them on.

He threw a spent cigarette into the fire and lit another.

It cheered up that dismal downstairs room where they lived. They lit up nice and it was okay, till they caught. Dil, she shouted, the tree! and she carried Mark to the far end of the room. The flames were going on one side on the low branches. And he picked the tree up low down on the trunk and ran out the front door with it and across the road to the gap in the railings. The wind fanned it and it got going properly, crackling, all that resin. The whole thing was one flame when he threw it down the bank the other side of the railings. The branches flailed and it stopped rolling and died into black.

Mark's father had told him about the Gold Rush before the film started. They struck gold in the Yukon and then everybody went there to find some. You could see why it was a Christmas film because of all the snow. It was a bit boring at first but it got better when Charlie Chaplin was walking on icy cliffs and he never really saw how close the edge was but he never fell off and then a bear followed him for a bit but he never even saw it. It was a real bear, you could tell, and it was really close.

'Remember when I burned the tree?' Dil said.

She looked at him. 'Wha' tha' got to do with Bert?'

'Nothing.'

She looked back at the screen. 'Aye I remember. You silly bugger.'

'You silly bugger' Lee said under his hat.

'Dwn say that, darling' she said.

Charlie Chaplin's face was very white and when you saw his teeth they were less white than his face. You had to concentrate to follow the story. They were in a cabin up the mountain and there was a blizzard. It was clever how they did the wind without any sound. There was a rag nailed across the bottom of the door and all the time it was fluttering. When they opened the door snow blew in and Charlie Chaplin had to run to stay in the same place and then he got blown out the other door. Somebody ought to come and rescue them but nobody did. Mark watched Charlie Chaplin turn into a giant chicken and he laughed a bit. Charlie Chaplin and the other man stranded in the cabin were cold and starving, and the other man, Big Jim, wanted to eat him. That's why he turned into a giant chicken. Charlie Chaplin ate a candle and he put salt on it. They were cold and starving and waiting to be saved and the cabin was almost falling apart in the wind. It was quite funny.

'Dwn worry' Dil said. 'You did more than many would.'

'Uh?'

'Going to see Bert.'

She thought of the unreachable old man. There were no words for it. 'Tha' bloody pokey little hole he do live in' she said at last. 'He got nothing and nobody. Just a couple o photos o people who didn' even know him. I'm a fool.'

Dil looked at her and then back at the puzzling shapes on the screen. 'No' he said.

Later on Charlie Chaplin got to a town with one foot bandaged up because he'd eaten his shoe, and it was pretty boring for a bit then. Every time the dancing woman Georgia came on there was a caption card with 'Georgia' on it and a picture of a flower and the music changed. She was cruel to Charlie Chaplin in front of her friends, but you could tell she didn' mean it.

Lee shifted his weight on his mother, settling towards sleep. 'Burp've got a bloody cat' he said. 'He's gwnna die.'

'Dwn say bloody' she said. 'Bert's cat en gwnna die.'

'Not Burp's cat. Burp is gwnna die.'

She caressed his shoulder with one hand, a cigarette perched in the other. 'No-o' she said. 'We do love old Bert dwn we, Lee?'

Mark made a big sigh as if they were interrupting the film, talking all the time. It was a silent so it shouldn' matter but somehow it did.

'Yes he is' Lee said. 'He always told me that. Burp is gwnna die, like a snot.'

Dil watched the screen. The black and white shapes were dancing senselessly under the lemon light from the shaded lamp.

Invisible signals poured out of the sky and down a wire and through the dusty city of valves and circuits inside the set and they resolved into sound and light that made these shapes, this dancing. It all poured into the eyes and ears, as the whitish light poured over Mark's supine body still dead straight on the floor. Now and then Mark laughed. What at? What a trick, to be absorbed as he was. Dil stared at the screen as through a window at figures he couldn't reach or understand.

The works were a dirty kind of city, the cupolas and stacks and sheds and sidings like valves and circuits. Ore and coal and scrap poured in and mixed with fire and got turned into stuff, into order – coke and benzene and naphthalene, and steel. The opposite of burning somehow. If you concentrated you could understand it. The screen, the works. Good things.

With Len Holden, it hadn' been a flamethrower of course. He'd stood up at the wrong time, that was all. All of them on the top of the hill, dug in, and it was night, ten o'clock, thereabouts and the mortars started pounding. That for hours. Bloody hours. And a Very light went up so for a second or two you knew it was coming and then the assault came at us. It was dark after the flare died, but light from somewhere must have picked him out, Len. It wasn't a flamethrower, like I thought at first. Just a burst of fire ripped across his chest and it hit the pouches in his tunic with the phosphorus grenades. His arms flung out and for a moment I swear, his fingers curled up like a dancer posing and the grenades lit up. He lit up like a. Christ.

He watched the pale light licking over Mark on the floor, the wings of his elbows sticking out where he propped his head on his hands.

Mark laughed suddenly.

Dil saw the shapes on the screen become people again and the music came back. The stranded hill in the dark and all the dead men on it receded, shrank. It was over. Sixteen, yes sixteen years.

He felt the comfortable heat of the fire against his leg. Automatically he leaned forward and checked it. There was plenty on. He might not even need to chuck any more coke on tonight.

She flicked her cigarette end into the glow and he watched it vanish. He looked at her and realised that she'd been watching him.

'Tell 'ou wha" she said, 'I'll do the fire in the room tomorrow. I'll be up before the boys. I'll get up when you go to work. It'll be plenty early enough.'

He looked into her face. He wanted to say something. He wanted to say: *The only certain thing inside us is the dead.* He opened his mouth to say it but nothing came out.

He got to his feet and stepped over Mark and went into the hallway.

'Thanks' he said as he shut the door behind him.

Mark wiggled a bit and tutted. Cold air rolled over him before his father shut the door. He heard the front door click open. That meant more draught.

Dil leaned against the jamb of the front door and pulled it half shut behind him. He realised how hot he was. He looked out into the dark and enjoyed the cold motionless air. The temperature had dropped.

It had been daylight before anybody came, after they'd beaten them back. Too late, and dead everywhere and Len a charred trunk. It was Indian soldiers got to them first. The First and Second Hyderabads. Then they could pull back.

He looked up at the streetlight outside the garden wall making a wan patch on the darkness. The stillness was good.

The cold was good. He stared into it.

The film got better again when Big Jim turned up in the town and he'd lost his memory and he needed Charlie Chaplin to help him find the gold. They were back up the mountain in the cabin and it got blown away on the ice and snow and it was rocking on the edge of a cliff and you'd think they'd get killed and they didn' know what was going on and it was funny. And then they were millionaires on a big ship and you could tell Charlie Chaplin was rich because of his coat and he was wearing a top hat. Then he put his bowler hat on for a photograph and Georgia turned up and she didn' know he was rich but she still liked him and they kissed so the film finished.

With the final music she tried to gather Lee up. His eyes were still open but he was only half there.

'Well tha' was a bit o fun' she said to Mark. Then, 'Come on, Dai. Bedtime, long gone.'

'Well well' Lee said.

Dil put his head round the living room door. 'I think it might be trying to snow' he said.

Suddenly animated, Mark scrabbled to his feet and dodged past him to the front door. His father turned and the two stood on the threshold. He heard his mother switching the television off. All the light would collapse into a silver dot and then vanish after a bit.

She lifted Lee onto her hip even though he was getting to be a big lump and stood with Mark and her husband.

The white light of the hallway fell a short distance across the path, then it was dark. Where the land fell away into the valley beyond their road, down towards Stanley Street and then the town, no lights showed. There was the one lamp-post outside their house and then it was ages down the road before the next. Mark liked the streetlight. The concrete had a nice way of curving at the top, and there was a bulb, like the ordinary bulbs in the house, with clear glass, but a bit bigger, pointing down under a dishshaped glass hood. When it was switched off you could even see the element, delicate and exact inside the bulb.

It was colder, but there was nothing falling past the lamp, and the path outside the door was dry.

'It was trying to a minute ago anyway' his father said.

'You silly old bugger' his wife said.

This time Lee said nothing.

'I hope it don't' she said. 'You got work tomorrow.'

'Mam!' Mark said. She shouldn' wish it away. He concentrated on the streetlight and stepped out on the doorstep. The cold went through his socks. He looked up. The light from the lamppost didn' reach the light from their door. There was mainly dark and then small islands of light.

She thought about the morning. Perhaps she'd get half an hour to herself after she lit the fires, then a nice day with the boys. Plenty o chicken left. She'd put Bert out of her mind for a day at least. She could do that sometimes, like she did with other things, like she did that morning on the hill.

Sometimes you had to. When Dil was off after Boxing Day she would go down and see him. She'd heard of Home Helps finding people. She didn' want to leave it too long.

Lee's head sank against her shoulder and the hat pushed loose.

Soon Dil would get the clock from the mantelpiece to take it to bed for the alarm in the morning, but before that he'd knock a bit more coal up for the fires. He didn' even have to light them, and day after tomorrow he had a couple of days off. Work hadn' been bad that day. There was one sticker when they were pushing an oven, but it had come okay with the rods. It was satisfying to see the hot wall of coke crumbling into the hopper wagons. Nobody got hurt. All of us warm and all of us fed, none come to harm and nobody dead. It was even pleasant to be in work on quieter days like this, making something.

Mark kept concentrating. His feet were tingling. The explosion of warmth and colour would continue yet. Boxing Day was almost as good as Christmas day. There were Korky the Cat's strange eyes and the patterns of bright colour in the annuals, the tree lights making coloured fingers on the branches through the plastic petals. In the morning Alexander Selkirk would still be standing at the top of the hill on his island. Perhaps he'd escape or perhaps the other soldiers would save him and at first they wouldn' understand what he said but then they'd talk and talk. He'd do a drawing of it like the drawing in the annual.

And Mark's horse, with a white blaze on his face and not like the horse in Bert's photo, would be waiting tied to a tree. But for now it was still Christmas day and he still hadn' gone to bed and his father had seen a snowflake and any second a piece of silver could come out of the blackness and glitter in the pale sphere of the lamplight.

THE ENTHUSIAST

A hand on my shoulder stopped me dead.

'Do you know a feller called Paul Fuller?'

I looked round. It was Roger Bayliss, hailing me as if we were old mates. I should have known his slightly breathy voice, his habitual briskness.

'Hello, Roger' I said.

We were on the steps going in to the building where we both work. There's only one door apart from the fire escape, yet I hardly ever see Bayliss. He and Chris Johns share an office a floor up from mine. He takes the lift, I take the stairs. Sometimes I glimpse him as the brushed-steel doors slide shut like a crematorium curtain and we nod as each of us vanishes. Once in a bluish moon I see him in a meeting, but not to talk to. On alternate blue moons we may cross in the cafe for a few moments and exchange cynicisms. He's thick-set, shortish, with receding fair hair. Thick glasses. A year or two younger than I am.

We stopped outside the building. The entrance is on a courtyard, away from the noise of traffic. The automatic door stood open. There were some smokers outside. The foyer looked gloomy as a cave.

'I was in school with a bloke called Paul Fuller' I said.

We each had a foot on a concrete step. We were either side of a handrail and he still had his hand on my shoulder, somewhere between being pally and making an arrest. He removed it. 'Wonder if it's the same feller. Where you from originally?'

I named the town, not that many miles away.

Roger commutes over the bridge from England, a long journey every day. I don't think he knows much about anywhere round here except for this building, our labs ten miles away, the cafe, and the pub a street away we take workleavers to for their sendoffs.

'Must be the same feller I reckon. He remembers you.'

'Common names.'

'Still, age and place, ey?'

His breathiness, or a little hoarseness in his voice, perhaps along with the telegraphic speech that always strikes me as phoney, give the impression that he's out of shape. And he is literally out of shape. He's one of these people who start almost pointy at the top of the head and get wider as they go down. His neck's wider than his balding crown, and he goes on getting broader, like a squat artillery shell. Yet he spends ages in the gym, gets on treadmills and runs nowhere for hours. Then he takes the lift.

He looked decisively over his glasses. 'Got to be.'

'We were friends for a bit' I said. 'Then he left. His dad got a job or something, quite early on. They left town.'

'Well he lives just by me. I have a drink with him now and then. He remembers you. I've known him years. Funny how your name didn't come up earlier. Anyway, nice feller.'

'He was a nice boy, Paul. Keen sort of a character. We were friends for a bit. He even wrote to me once after he left. We were still kids. I came across the letter a while back.'

'Exceptionally nice bloke. Like I say, we go to the pub now and then. Some Sundays.'

'I haven't seen him since. I can't think. He moved away when I was. I don't know how old. Young anyway.'

We stood each side of the handrail each with a foot on the next step. I looked at Roger Bayliss's fiftyish bullet head, his open half smiling mouth, and he looked not quite through and not quite over his glasses. I thought of Paul Fuller, a schoolboy. Would he even have been in his teens when I saw him last?

'Anyway, look.' Bayliss tapped my shoulder again. 'Tell you what, I'm sure he'd like to be in touch. I'll send you his email.'

He did his trick of hurtling away, through the open door and towards the lift, as if I'd stopped him in the urgent out-of-breath work he had to do somewhere else.

*

Paul Fuller lived in the next street down the hill from us on the estate. It was a fifties council estate built in stages. As one political party after another promised to build more houses at each election they'd shave the cost of building, so our house had lower ceilings and smaller rooms than the

69

ones two streets below. Some late additions to our street in the sixties had front rooms so shallow you could almost touch the back wall and the front window simultaneously with your arms outstretched. Obscurely, we had the idea that the further up the mountain your street was the harder you got. Ours was the second street from the top. Beyond that, beyond a long concrete drainage ditch that we often played in when it was dry, was almost featureless mountain, with oozy peat bog and bulrushes, scabby circular depressions of dry-lichened limestone rubble. My parents called the street above ours Up Around, and Up Around was a place we were mildly warned not to hang about in, because it was a shade harder than our street. But it always looked okay when I passed through it. The estate looked down and east across the valley, to old terraces and pine plantations, and, for most of my childhood, till it was cleared and grassed over, to the hundreds of acres of blackish tip wreckage around the site of an old colliery, shut and demolished a generation before I was born.

Paul's house was in a cul-de-sac below us and a bit grander than ours, but without our grandstand view of the town. He lived in a right-side semi and I lived in a left-side semi, so even though we were in different streets I had an odd sense of our houses mirroring one another.

How had I met him? I couldn't remember. Our parents didn't know one another. I don't think we went to the same primary school. Perhaps we did. Am I making this up? It's like remembering a dream, where the effort to reassemble it in the waking mind provokes invention. But say Paul went to Duke Street School. I went to Charlestown. Like the fear and suspicion of Up Around there was fear and suspicion between schools. We'd chant when we saw Duke Street kids

Duke Street, Duke Street, sittin on the wall
Charlestown, Charlestown, best of all.

They were rough in Duke Street School all right. All of us in Charlestown knew that.

Somehow, in the invisible networks of childhood, we met before we were both sent to the same comp when we were eleven. I find myself remembering, inventing, a conversation with Paul that liberalised my view of humanity.

'What's Duke Street like, then?' I say.

'It's okay' Paul says.

I must have had that conversation with some kid or other.

Except Paul perhaps would have enthused. He had one of those triangular faces, broad at the top of the head, narrowing sharply along the cheeks to the chin. His ears stuck out a little at their top edges, which added to the effect. It was as if he was going somewhere, pointing the way he would take. This much persists perfectly. He had an open face. His eyes, I think, must have been blue. His hair was straight and brown with the fringe of most childhoods, and like me he was thin.

But yes, he would have enthused about Duke Street if that

was where he went. Miss So and So would have been great. Mr So and So would have been strict but really interesting. It was what he did. Paul was keen on things. The trait, condition, is crystal to me as the face, even if circumstance, event and sequence aren't.

The way to Paul's house was downhill and therefore on the way somewhere, from cool to warm, from apparent nothing to apparent something. It was just a few steps off the path we took every day to go to school or to town in the valley below. To us, footpaths, mostly unofficial and beaten ad hoc by the feet of children and sheep, were more significant than mere roads. When Poole, our new Geography teacher, asked us to draw a map of how we got to school when I was eleven, I, who was good at drawing, was defeated. It was the impossible web of journeys on foot, on improvised secret paths, that I tried to compress into a map. When my father, who couldn't draw for toffee, sketched it out swiftly I was amazed and saw that the footways and turns of the fugitive map in my mind weren't there at all. They couldn't be squeezed into the almost closed interstices of the roads and streets he'd drawn. It was accurate, efficient, and an annihilation of the world I knew.

Yet I don't think I called very often at Paul's house. For him to see me he had to make an effort. Even to go up the mountain he didn't have to pass my house. Still he often did call.

One day I think he called with the invitation to come out to play that belonged to our lore and he enthused about a shed in his back garden. I'd never seen his back garden then. I don't remember if we went there straight away. I remember suddenly being in it with Paul and some other boys. One of them was probably Colin who lived near Paul. I'd been in Colin's house, which seemed very clean and new, and I remember that over the fireplace in the front room there was a portrait of a champion racing pigeon. It was under glass and seemed like a painting, but perhaps it was a touched-up photograph. There was some sort of prize plaque for the bird on the mantelpiece like a medal mounted on a wooden shield. This made me think the pigeon looked like a soldier with a dress-sword and a cocked hat. Somewhere, Colin's father must have had a rickety pigeon cote, perhaps in his back garden or maybe on the open mountain where some of the men built them, but I never saw it.

Paul's shed was made of bitumenised black corrugated iron. It had no windows and it was so low that even we could only just stand up in it with our heads pressed against the timbers under the almost flat tin roof. It had a beaten earth floor. There might have been some chicken wire and old feathers lying around. The door too was corrugated tin on a timber frame. Paul tugged it open and pulled it shut with impressive competence. Intense white daylight leaked through tiny pinholes in the metal.

In a story something dark would happen at this point. But it didn't. What did we play in there? I recall nothing except that we had stumps of candles. Playing with fire, like going

Up Around, was something warned against, and we were good boys. So this was really something. The dark of the shed, like a power cut, legitimised the striking of a match. There must have been that thrill of the discovery of the cartoonish elasticity of our own shadows, the plastic qualities of heated wax, the fishtail blur of the yellow tip of a candleflame, the way the warm light could lick your hand gentler than a dog, the way it could darken a patch on the underside of the tin roof.

So the warnings about fire, like the warnings about Up Around and about kids who went to Duke Street, were simplifications. The lick on the hand was a friendly tickle. When Paul held the candle stump to the roof we watched how the friendly tongue magicked an intenser velvet black patch on the scabby metal and then started to blister. Our faces were lit up around it, Paul's impartial but rapt, and showing nothing proprietorial to us, his invited guests.

Another exotic thing about Paul was that he had a grandfather who lived next door. I didn't have any grandfathers, just like I didn't have a shed. I had had one, who remained only in one wisp of memory. I was unable to deduce that there'd been a second who'd died before I was born. But I made no connection between the vaporous memory and the man who lived next door to Paul.

'Come and meet my Gransha' I suppose he must have said sometime, in a voice that leaned high and expressive on the key words, with a habitual urgency.

Paul's grandfather, I realise now, looked a bit like Paul, with an only slightly blunted triangular head, broad at the top, with ears sticking out a little as if on the alert, lips parted a little, and eyes lively. But he was almost hairless which made him very pink, and most impressively he wore his raincoat indoors all the time, with the belt done up. He talked to us a lot but I have no idea what about. His house had less carpet than ours and more lino. And he had an astonishing television set from some ancient time. He sat awkwardly in an uncomfortable-looking armchair right next to this machine, and he needed to. It was a small brown box. The tiny screen bulged hemispherically into the room as if it were a small goldfish bowl that had been crammed into a strange cupboard. The thick glass gave a greenish tinge to the few smudgy monochrome lines which, if you stared hard enough, turned into blurred images of drowning people opening their mouths.

I don't think Paul was my best friend. I spent more time with Dai Thomas next door to us, whose house had one downstairs room with no furniture or carpet, who liked nature and proved it by knowing about breeds of dogs and cutting the legs off a live frog while I watched one day in that concrete drainage ditch, or with Gwyn James, a street away, with whom I drew comics sometimes and with whom, a few years later, I would get catastrophically drunk quite often. But mostly I played and walked on my own.

Still, Paul and I intersected regularly on the invisible, unofficial paths, and, I realise, he sought me out sometimes.

*

After Roger stopped me on the steps that day, the official tracks of my work life went on while these half obliterated tracks of memory wound intermittently among them. I'm one of those rare people who enjoys their job, and the work on hydrogenation was keeping me busy. The elastic shadows appeared only fitfully. Streams of moments, places, states of mind, came occasionally, but nothing you could call a narrative. They were connected purely perhaps because of age and place, each to the next as arbitrarily as the different colours of a chain of handkerchiefs pulled from a conjuror's pocket.

Bayliss never sent me the email address and it never occurred to me to remind him.

*

It must have been a couple of months later – I don't think I'd seen Bayliss at all in the meantime – when I got this email at work

Dear Rob,
Roger Bayliss told me he works with you. I hope you don't mind me getting in touch with you again after a long time. It's a very long time since that day I bumped into you in the Lifeboat. I think you were meeting your girlfriend. Are you still in touch with her? I see Roger now and then. He's a good mate. He told me about you. It's great that

you've done really well for yourself. Anyway, hello. I hope
all's well with you. Perhaps we can keep in touch.
Paul (Fuller)

It had all the awkwardness of a message that had no content
except for the fact that it was a message. It made a noise in
my head like his remembered voice, a little high on the
emphasised words, somehow a little urgent. Of course that
could not be in the writing, only from something I remembered, or invented.

The Lifeboat was a pub in Cardiff. It's gone now. There
was a time when most of the buildings around it had been
pulled down and it stood on its own on waste ground, in a
grid of houseless streets.

Had I met him there? I'd been a student in Cardiff. I did
go to the Boat with a girlfriend sometimes. It was a good pub.
We must have been nineteen or twenty. Technically grown
up. The only time I could have met him in approximate
adulthood. How many years after he'd left our home town?
Six? Eight?

The conjuror tugged the handkerchief and another
coloured flag of cloth unfurled.

*

It was late afternoon, I think, or early evening, anyway not
all that dark yet. A heavily overcast day. I stepped in to the
pub through the glass door and it was busy and bright as

usual. Some man was coming towards me and I was trying to look round him to see if I could spot Amy. He'd recognised me and crossed the pub in my direction. When he got me to look at him he said, 'Rob' and I recognised him. He hadn't changed except for being taller and having longer hair. There was the tapering face, the quick eyes, the mouth slightly open. His voice – and this is probably wrong – was unchanged too. He was carrying something, a rucksack, a packed nylon rucksack on an aluminium frame. He had an arm through a shoulder strap. The rucksack hung heavily at a skewed angle. There was an emptied pint in the other hand, foam sliding down its walls.

Good god. We said one another's name again. How many years? Last time was when? On the uphill side of our teens.

How was I?

I was fine, how was he?

He was great, yeah, really good.

I was doing Chemistry in Cardiff. This girl.

I looked round for Amy. I must have looked a bit anxious, or preoccupied anyway. It was busy but I didn't think she was there yet.

He'd left school early, after they advised him not to stay on for the sixth form.

He told me this stuff and I half listened.

Paul was the sort of boy everybody knew was bright but he never did that well in school. It should have frustrated him but it never seemed to.

He'd started a sort of apprenticeship in a factory then left. Anyway, he was off somewhere, to do a course on something. On his way there now. It sounded great. He was looking forward.

We were standing near the door. He didn't put his other arm through the strap. He held on to the empty glass for a moment, hesitated, then put it on one of those shelves they have round pillars in pubs.

Amy might have come in the other way.

We didn't shake hands. People didn't much in those days.

It was great to see me.

Yes, it was.

And it must have been evening after all, because as the glass door swung shut when he went out, the sky, turbulent with grey cloud like a sea, was going dark.

*

This shadow, or flag, or path, whatever it was, hadn't existed till I sat there in my office staring at Paul's email. It was after all a feeble postscript. And I realised suddenly why I remembered his face that well. It wasn't because of the Lifeboat. I think I barely looked at him there. When I glanced at him in the pub it was the eleven year old that came, and comes, back with extraordinary clarity.

Whether we went to the same primary or not, when we got to the comprehensive school together, for just the first term we were in the same class. The lower school of the comp was a late Victorian building, like my old primary, but it smelled a lot worse and had a spider's web of outbuildings – extra classrooms added ad hoc that got less solid the further they were from the main building. It was in an alien part of town, down in the valley, to which we were bussed.

Education, that thing my father held up as all hope, got complicated. It was broken into pieces and scattered among these different buildings with different teachers. We wore black uniforms, and electric bells rang and we had to walk from one building to another. We were graded like eggs or wool and constantly shuffled from one container to another. In so far as we played any part in this grading, I turned out to be good at it and got Moved Up to a better class just after Christmas, which must have been when Paul and I stopped being in the same class.

In that first term, Art was in one of the less awful sheds that made up half the school. It wasn't all that cold and it was spacious and light, and I was good at Art. Even though Poole had shaken me with the impossibility of drawing a map of how I got there, I still knew I was good at this. So one more handkerchief unfolds from the pocket, the only definite one with me and Paul in the same classroom.

I sat next to him in an Art lesson. Though this was the thing I loved above everything else, the art teacher – her name's gone – terrified us. She was probably young. When you're eleven you can't tell. To me the girls in the next year up were grown women, as proved by their mesmeric breasts and the hints of bras through their bri-nylon shirts, and by their clean fingernails. The art teacher hated us.

There were only two columns of paired desks in this long room, with, instead of an aisle between them, what seemed a gulf. It seemed arranged for cheerlessness. In memory it looks like a counting house in an old film. She sat at the front, of course, at a central desk, said as little as she could, and then spoke almost inaudibly, never smiled, moved only when she had to, and then moved slowly.

I sat with Paul towards the back of one of these columns of desks. The air of fear made the opening of the lesson silent and tense. Without explanation, she made us all lift our desks and turn them and our chairs sideways so that we faced our neighbour. We moved the furniture in an odd silence, as if in some deadly, rhythmless folkdance, and waited. With the spontaneity of a hired mourner she walked up and down the aisle, which was slightly reduced in width by the altered furniture, and gave us each a large sheet of thick greyish paper. Paul was sitting on the inner side, in the gulf, facing out. I was facing in. We had to draw a picture of the person opposite. For me this was great. I loved the bite of the pencil onto paper and the figuring of that blankness into shapes and spaces. In spite of how the failed map must have stung me, I was still enough of a child not to be cowed by the impossibility of realising someone else's face.

The line could lasso spaces which like magic stopped being gaps and turned into stuff. The mass of an eye or a collar. But then the line could become the stuff itself when you wanted it to, like doing the strands of the hair or when you shaded in. You could make the line different so that it turned from a boundary into material. And there were tricks too. Most people thought that your eyes were closer to the top of your head than to your chin but this wasn't true. If you drew an egg shape the eyes were on an invisible line about half way along it. It was a kind of system. Everybody was more or less the same. The more bit was easier. The less bit was hard to capture.

It was then that I must have looked hard at the map of Paul's face. The broadness at the crown of the head will have appeared, the vee to the chin. The ears sticking out a little at their tops, and the asymmetry there, one sticking out more than the other by a fraction. I remember that the lips were parted a little, the eyes direct.

In the American comics I copied with Gwyn James there was a system for doing eyes. You did an arching line for the top lid and three quarters of a disc under it for the iris and pupil. That was all. You didn't need to bother with the lower lid. And in Physics when you had to draw an eye receiving light rays in a diagram it was always a side view like a sort of hieroglyph. You just did a sort of vee on its side like opened compasses with an arc joining the arms. But that day I must have looked and tried to notate the individual details of the thickness of the lids, the strands of the lashes. There was the subtle bony lump in the middle of the nose too.

Had this taken as long as half an hour? When I emerged from my picture and looked around, the funereal room reappeared with its small embarrassed noises. Some of the others looked as if they'd finished a while ago and had their arms folded. And there was Paul, working at his own picture. Because he had sort of vanished while I'd been staring at him so hard.

I looked from my drawing to him and back again. I'd expected it to be good enough to show off about, but to something like my astonishment it actually looked like him. I don't know whether I realised then that a good likeness doesn't necessarily make a good picture, but anyway my surprise was empty of any pride or delight. It was just surprise. Almost a shock.

I looked around again. The world was unchanged. The teacher began to reprise her dead march along the gulf, this time slowing to look at each picture.

I watched her face when my turn came. She didn't look at me. Her eyes flickered over the picture. Two seconds passed. Her mourner's expression didn't change. She didn't look at Paul. She said nothing and went on to the next desk.

Of the picture Paul made of me I recall nothing. It occurred to me then looking at his email that his unofficial map or chain of handkerchiefs or whatever it was might be quite different from mine. He might not connect me with the shed or with the drowning figures through the porthole of his Gransha's antiquated television. He would of course connect me with the sounds and smells of my own spaces. Perhaps with the glacial red and cream plastic of the three piece suite in our best room – The Room my mother called it – that we sometimes played in, looking through my older sister's records. The Room was always cold, except for Christmas when my father lit the tiny fire. Or perhaps he'd remember having to keep quiet in the day when my father was asleep after a night-shift. How different our shared pasts were.

The art teacher never put the portraits on the wall. There was little wall space in that hut, with its acres of draughty windows. I realise now that conditions were almost as bad for the teachers as they were for us. The drawing was probably crude. But the bright flag of my small amazement is perhaps what fixed Paul's face in my mind, and it recurred in my belated recognition when he spotted me and made towards me in the Lifeboat.

*

I stared at the few lines of his email on the monitor and sensed the packed unknowable freight of memory behind the apparently empty words.

I wrote

Dear Paul,

Thanks for your mail. It's great to hear from you.

I deleted it and started again

Dear Paul,

How good to hear from you

I deleted that. A phrase I may use now, but we never used an exclamatory 'How' as kids. 'How clever!' or 'How thrilling!' was the language of children in Enid Blyton books. We might have said 'That's clever' or 'There's good'.

I settled for

Dear Paul,

It's great to hear from you.

Yes, Roger mentioned that he knew you. Thanks for reminding me about The Boat in Cardiff. That must be well over 30 years ago now. How did the course go? You were on your way to one that day weren't you? It's almost a lifetime but it feels like nothing. I live in the Vale now. Married, one daughter, more or less grown up. (The daughter, that is.) How are you and what have you been up to?

Yes, let's keep in touch. If you're ever up this way you must call in.

Regards,

Rob

I read over this miserable rubbish and deleted *It's almost a lifetime but it feel like nothing* and the word *Regards*. He hadn't put in a sign-off word, so I didn't either.

When I hit Send, I noticed it was barely four minutes

since I'd read Paul's email. An interstice. I had a lot to do.
The day's work rose and closed over me.

*

It was two weeks or a little longer before Paul wrote back.

Dear Rob,
Great to hear from you. I did do that course.
(I had to scroll back over the emails to find out what this
meant.)
It was great, an important step, not quite the way I've gone
since but sort of pointing the way. Electronics has changed,
you don't need me to tell you. Anyway, it set me on the
road to computing and that was it for me. IT was it! Sort
of flukey but it was great. I got in more or less at the start
of it all and I've been all round the world helping set up
systems and advising. Nowadays you don't even need to
travel to do that so I got the best of it. Anyway, I got to the
point where I could actually take early retirement, so I
have. It's great. It irritates and upsets my wife on many
levels (two sons, by the way, also irritated), as you can
imagine, but I'm pretty good with it.
Anyway, no, I haven't been "home" as you call it much if
ever. I was barely thirteen when I left. I imagine it's
changed quite a bit. It's all a bit of a blur.
We're quite close to the Channel here. From the end of
my street you can look across and see it raining in South

86

Wales. I can spot it from the bedroom too. The lights are nice at night.

Anyway, great we're in touch.

Paul

I didn't answer straight away. Work was hectic.

The development work on hydrogenation of vegetable oils kept me engrossed. It's used for making spreads and butter substitutes. You sparge hydrogen with a catalyst through the oil at high temperature and thicken it, transform it by degrees into different kinds of fat and control its melt range, all its qualities. I enjoyed overseeing the tests, now that I no longer did the donkey work in the lab, calibrating the variables of temperature and catalyst with tightening control through reaction after reaction, almost getting the stuff to be whatever they wanted. And my daughter was getting married.

Though making a pile and getting out early was something people talked about, I never wished for it. Still, somehow I felt – overtaken It seemed to me you had to be somebody, good or bad, to get out as early as Paul had. Retiring early was for dodgy chief constables, or for the crooked dentists who'd drilled and filled our healthy teeth for cash all through our childhoods. But it was merely an ambiguous twinge. It was of no great moment.

*

So he'd been barely thirteen. I had no recollection of his actually leaving town, though some details around it remain. They moved only a few miles away at first, to the next valley, beyond the mountain opposite us, beyond the terraces and pine plantations, and close to the steelworks. But to us it was an immensity. When I told my father where the Fullers had moved to – Paul had made a point of giving me the address – he tossed his head and said, 'Christ almighty, that's a bigger bloody hole than this is.'

I always thought my father was joking when he talked like this. I didn't think where we lived was a bloody hole.

Paul had gone to a small estate near the steelworks called City Gardens.

Some time he'd said, 'You'll have to come over. It's really interesting.'

I don't know how I got there, but I did go once. Perhaps I made some convoluted bus journeys or perhaps Paul's father had a car by then. I think I would have remembered the car, so it was almost certainly bus.

All this came to me on my way to the photocopier when I crossed Roger Bayliss's path. He was carrying a sheaf of printed pages and bustling past me with a nod.

'Thanks for giving Paul my email' I said.

'What?' He slowed in his trajectory and looked at me.

He looked puzzled. I could see his mind catching up. He turned to face me as he passed into the corridor, walking sideways a few steps and waving the papers to indicate his urgency.

'Did I?' he said. 'Paul. Right. Oh, glad you're touch. Haven't seen him recently. Wish him my best.' Wagging the papers, he vanished.

I got the impression that he hadn't passed the address on at all. Perhaps Paul had looked it up.

I turned to the photocopier.

City Gardens was a cluster of a few semidetached council houses outside the steelworks town. There was no city, but the houses had small gardens of sorts. It was sunny and cold. The little estate was impressive to me because it wasn't so godforsakenly far up a mountain as where I lived. It was on a very steep hill, but the huge roadless ridge that separated it from our town rose above it. Below it in the valley bed was the tangled machinescape of the heavy end of the steelworks. The pavements were a little gritty underfoot with pollution.

Paul and I greeted one another like strangers. In his living room there was a young coal fire burning in the buff ceramic grate. Amazingly, right next to the chimney breast there was a window and through it, below us, the blast furnaces were smouldering. I remember looking from the yellowish smoke coming off the freshly lit coal to the smoking retorts of the furnaces.

That moment, I'd thought, had been the last time I'd seen him till he reminded me about the Lifeboat. I'd never understood why they moved and it never occurred to me to wonder what had happened to his grandfather and the strange television.

Suddenly somehow the blast furnaces plucked another handkerchief from the pocket. I could see Paul's house not in City Gardens but the one he'd left, a street away from my own.

We're in his kitchen, the mirror of the kitchen of my house, and there's cold sunlight pouring through the window above the sink and on the windowsill is a goldfish in a bowl. Am I inventing this out of the memory of his Gransha's telly? I don't think so, because on some other day there's a bloom of brilliant green algae in the water, which Paul changes with magic competence while I watch. The green sludge is gone and there's clarity again. The bowl is one of those old-fashioned spherical ones, like in a cartoon. Was it really there? The goldfish is quite large with a willowy arrangement of fins that don't look much use for getting anywhere.

That day of cold sunlight – we must have been about eleven – the bowl was clear, a kind of lens, and lit with the articulated mirrors of the drifting goldfish so that you might mistake it for warmth. We were carrying a large flat box. We took it into Paul's mother's equivalent of The Room, the room which in Dai Thomas's house was empty. Paul's Room was more like ours. It was neat, with sparse furniture and a thin carpet with polished tiles showing round the edge.

We put the chemistry set on the carpet. It was quite an old set. I can't remember where we got it. On the lid there was an outdated picture of a man wearing a tie and a veenecked sleeveless pullover and a boy with a short back and sides and an unnaturally white shirt. With a gloved hand the man was holding up a glass flask which glowed with some unspecified material and lit up their openmouthed and wonderstruck faces. Inside, the set had a few cheap bits of equipment slotted into yellow card. There were some test tubes, one of toughened glass, a tiny flask, much smaller than the one in the picture, and a fan of corked, labelled test tubes of chemicals, some still sealed with some kind of coloured wax. There was even a flimsy Bunsen burner, but no retorts. The tubes contained coloured crystals and powders and stuff that looked like coloured stone and even some lumps of metal. There were names on the labels and chemical symbols.

Paul prised a tube from the yellow card. It was about half full with some bright orange rock and dust. The label said 'Mercuric Oxide'.

We were doing Chemistry in school by then in a cold portakabin that smelled of newish wooden benches and sometimes of gas and unidentifiable substances. It had pointlessly uncomfortable high stools instead of chairs, with handslots in the seats that hurt when you sat on them. I can't remember Paul being there, but I suppose he must have been. We called the teacher Lurch, after The Addams Family on television because he was tall and cadaverous. When he smiled his face was whiter than his teeth. He was better than most of the teachers but he hit a boy once when the boy said 'You rang?' to him in a slow deep voice, which was the television Lurch's catchphrase.

'What a great colour' Paul said. '*Mercuric Oxide*. So that means this is made out of mercury and oxygen.'

We stared at the orange stuff, wondering.

'Mercury?' I said. 'How can there be mercury in there?'

We knew mercury from the silver thread in thermometers. Lurch had told us about how an old scientist with a moustache, Torricelli, had latched on to the mercury barometer. He used a column of mercury going up and down in a glass tube as the air pressure changed and almost by accident showed that the old idea *nature abhors a vacuum* was wrong. It was the first time I heard the word *abhor*. When the mercury went down in the sealed tube he made a vacuum at the top and amazed everybody.

Except, Lurch said, the old idea was sort of right because pressure tends to fill the spaces. The old blokes were just wrong to think it was impossible to create emptiness. It was just difficult. Lurch had a plastic bottle of mercury in his stockroom. It contained about half a pint. He passed it round one day for us to test its weight. He told us it was thirteen and a half times denser than water. Heavier than lead. Like you lot, he said, it's relatively dense. When I got home I got an empty milk bottle and poured six and three quarter pints of water into a bucket and picked it up. I tried to imagine it all being pressed down into half a pint. Once, we got blobs of mercury somewhere when Lurch was out of the room and blew them round the bench with a straw. They were tiny racing impervious liquid mirrors. That day he passed the half-pint bottle round it looked dull and trapped in the translucent plastic. He told us the old name was *quicksilver*. I thought of the racing droplets on the bench top but then he told us it didn't mean quick as in fast, but moving. It was just an old word for *alive*.

'But it's, like, orange. Like rock' I said to Paul, in his Room.

We stared some more.

It was Paul who made the breakthrough. 'The thing is' he said, 'oxygen burns, right?'

I agreed.

'It supports combustion' he said, quoting Lurch. Lurch said memorable things. 'So if we burn this stuff we'll burn the oxygen off, and we'll get some proper mercury.' He looked at me and his face lit. 'Ding!'

'You rang' I said.

It seems to me that we spent all the hours left in the day trying to burn the oxygen out of a chunk of that mercuric oxide. We teased a piece of the orange rock out of the phial and into the toughened test tube. Paul searched the kitchen for a while looking for a gas nozzle to which he could attach the rubber hose of the Bunsen burner. There wasn't one. He held a lit match under the tube and the glass blackened and nothing happened. He lit a candle stump and fixed it on an old saucer on a hardened slurry of old wax. He got a glove somewhere and held the tube over the candleflame with that and we looked at the mercuric oxide doing very little. We beamed our willpower through the smoky glass to get some of the dust in the bottom of the tube to do *something*. Perhaps it did sort of simper and stir, but perhaps we imagined it. We gave that up and wiped the smokeblack off, leaving a dark starburst on a teatowel. Then Paul got some kind of tongs and held the tube over the gas jet on the cooker hob. We waited and waited. The gas jet flickered its complicated blue and violet tongues. We knew from Lurch which part of the flame was the hottest. Slowly the mercuric oxide began to do things. It shifted a little and went black and then softened its edges and went a bit gooey. This was it. It would work. We watched and watched and nothing changed further. After a while I wandered into Paul's Room and looked into the open box on the floor. *Lead. Alum. Anhydrous Copper Sulphate.* The different textures and densities playing dead, captured and waiting to be transformed.

I went back into the kitchen. Paul's lively eyes, a little dulled, were still fixed on the blackened chip in the test tube. He moved it away from the flame and passed it under his nose, sniffing. 'Poo. He said. If that's oxygen.' He waited some more and we kept staring.

At last Paul summed up our conclusions pithily.

'Aw shit to it' he said, and turned the gas off.

He carried the tube before him up the garden and tried to knock the blackened stuff on the place where his father tipped the ashes from the fire. Most of it fell out but some of it was welded inside the tube.

Days later he came up to me excitedly. 'Hey, I asked Lurch about the mercury. He looked a bit surprised when I told him we tried that. He said it did ought to work only we probly had to burn it like a lot hotter, like really get it really really hot. He said not to do it mind. Think of that though.'

We imagined the transformation of the red rock, a globule of pure mercury distilling and cohering in some shimmering white crucible.

And I thought of an old Rupert annual my sister had given me. In one story Rupert Bear went to see the Wise Old Goat in wintry mountains, where he had an industrial plant hidden in a mountain with an enormous lens and tundish mounted at an angle like a telescope through which he distilled sunbeams into jars. Rupert skis back down the mountain with a bag full of these glowing jars slung over his shoulder on a pole, and they resurrect his mother from her winter illness. But I didn't tell Paul about that.

*

I must have tapped my security code into the photocopier without realising it. I was watching the scanning flash of the copier and the pages of some document were peeling one by one into the tray. From the corridor outside I could hear the hydraulics of the lift start up as Roger Bayliss returned to his office.

In fact it should have been about five hundred centigrade to get mercury. And perhaps Lurch was being circumspect not to mention it or perhaps he didn't know how poisonous the vapour was that we'd started to create. It's even possible we had teased a little mercury from the rock and couldn't see it. It probably would have condensed in a tiny amount further up the wall of the test tube or sweated out of the air in a fine miasma.

Shortly after this I won an award in work for some of the hydrogenation work. Chris Johns sent me an email with my name as the title followed by 'PhD, StOaAC'. She congratulated me on this major achievement and the award, she said, was for Services To Obesity and Artery Clogging. It entailed going to a hotel in London and wearing a chest-puffing suit and, with a half a dozen of the team I directed, collect a significant handshake, an absurd photograph, and a small plaque. My daughter's wedding came and went.

*

But it was only a few days later that I wrote back.

In his email he'd put home in inverted commas. *"Home" as you call it.* This felt dissonantly both right and somehow slighting, but I put that out of my mind. I struggled to find things to say. I remember it slithering towards being like those circular letters some people send at Christmas giving all the good news about work and family as if it were a press release for a business or a pamphlet for an evangelical church. I tried to mention the run of the mill award and the matter of course wedding in passing, and then deleted them. There was no way of writing in an ironic shrug without it looking like an arch excuse for bragging. I put the wedding back in in as few words as possible. There was at least no direct self-aggrandisement in that.

Somewhere in the blether I said something like *You say I've done well for myself* – those words 'for yourself' had stuck in my mind – *but it sounds like you're way ahead of me. How well must you have done to be able to afford to bail out early? I can't contemplate retiring for at least a decade. Fluky or not, sounds like things worked out well for you.* I paused a long time. I felt how my 'for you' mirrored his 'for yourself'.

It was a Friday, a quiet day in work. I listened to the distant traffic. I wrote *And you probably did well not to go back home too.*

At first I put inverted commas around home as he had, then I deleted them.

I thought of the estate and the town in the years after Paul had left. The withdrawing tide of old industry, softly roaring, more or less orderly, taking the tracks up as it left. It wasn't good, but there was a kind of decency to it. Then, after I'd started my real working life elsewhere, making raids home during holidays, how at the end of the seventies change was catastrophically accelerated into destruction. To the muted soundtrack of the far road a stream of seething ideas and images ran through me. There was an economic vacuum that sucked a drug market into existence, a sudden, turned-on scorching heat that burned through the place like a furious disease. Except that it had been induced. It was someone's experiment, or perhaps an auto da fe. I thought of the husks of abandoned houses, of my mother a few years later, alone, growing old and ill, almost marooned on the mountain when the buses had been deregulated out of existence, of the scabmouthed young man who robbed her in the street one day. Had I been born a decade or two later I might have been him. I found seven words and typed *The 79 election was bad for us.* Us? I went on *I was away by then too, but the 80s were a disaster. The place is still recovering. You ought to take a look.* But I added that he probably knew all this, invited him again to visit us – another us – in the Vale. Neither Paul nor I had sent addresses or phone numbers. That would come, I supposed. I hesitated a bit and hit Send.

I don't know why I hesitated. Three pathetic sentences hid multitudes, or perhaps they were too much.

Our thoughts are sealed in a kind of emptiness. To the world they're silent and unknowable. Only in so far as they cause us to act or speak or not act or not speak, like the flickering or stillness of a needle, are they tenuously capable of a signal to the world. When I happen, as I rarely do, to look at the face, say, of Bayliss, I can see nothing of that inner partial vacuum where his mind persists. If I do see some tremor of the needles of a complex bank of dials through the glass of

his spectacles, my reading of them is just guesswork. We can
choose to act or to utter and so our thinking, in some mediated
way, perhaps, can be known. But how truthful the utterance
or act can be I don't know. Who's able to say what they think?
It may be an uncatchable quickness. Through the dense glass
of forty years, what attempts at mouthings were Paul and I
making to one another?

Anyway, I'd tried avoiding writing one of those circular
good news letters. Obscurely it felt like an admission of
weakness. *Disaster*. Really? Wasn't that word too big, too casu-
ally used? But then there were the trashed houses, the scabbed
mouth I'd omitted. The young man who could have been me,
whom I'd actually wanted to murder at one time, who wrecked
his own life in twenty minutes in a magistrates' court for fourteen pounds, for some tubes of glue or a can of butane.

All that in the half second before hitting Send. It wasn't
truly much like agonising after all. A moment only.

*

After my mother's death, ten years ago, I was with my sister
clearing the house when I found the letter Paul had written
to me, the one I mentioned to Bayliss. Paul must have sent it
after he'd left town, not long after I'd visited him in City
Gardens, with the blast furnaces and the yellow-smoky
fireplace. It was in a rubbish of papers in a small cardboard
suitcase, still in its envelope. Three small sheets of pale blue

paper – more handkerchiefs in the chain – matching the envelope, lightly feinted, written in blue fountain pen. It was the watermarked Basildon Bond stationery we used to use, imagining we were sophisticated. None of us had phones then. The letter was naively correct. Paul's address was in the top right corner of the first page, with all the commas painstakingly dotted and curled and the date underneath as we'd been taught. It was on one side of the paper only. He'd made an effort with his slightly clenched, not particularly neat handwriting, the cursive letters formed with laborious accuracy. On my knees at the opened suitcase, while my sister took clothes still on their hangers out of a wardrobe next to me, I noticed how the lower case eff was carefully pinched to a point at the top and bottom of each loop, how it hung almost precisely by its mid point on the feint-line.

But I can't remember exactly what it was about. It started

Dear Rob,

Hello!

It said something about how interesting his new school was, not as rough as we'd supposed it would be, and it talked about how good things were. Then it said

Anyway, the main reason I'm writing is, have you ever thought of joining – and I can't remember what came next. It was some club or movement that had meetings and 'activities' and trips. It wasn't the scouts. It had some specialism. I could get a bus to whatever it was, Paul said. Maybe astronomy or amateur acting or rock climbing or ping pong. It didn't matter what it was.

And somehow the swimming pool coloured paper brought the thought that this was typical Paul Fuller. My sister was folding the armfuls of dark coats and print dresses into a box to be given away or thrown away, and Paul was still signalling across decades, waving an arm for me to hurry up.

Whatever the club was I remember thinking, aged about thirteen, that it sounded crackbrained to me. I don't believe I ever answered.

Once, in work at a staff development session, an industrial psychologist told us that people have a finite number of close friendships they can make. He called them emotional arms. Say someone has three of these arms. If one of them loses its grip on a friend it waves emptily in the air till it finds another. A few people have dozens of such arms. Most people have a few. Some rare people have none at all and are content sealed in the vessel of themselves.

I couldn't help thinking of this as being like the valency of atoms, or the schoolboy version of it Lurch taught us, their capacity to combine with others expressed as a number. So hydrogen, the stuff the sun's largely made of, Lurch said, has a valency of one. Carbon, the substance we're largely made of, has a valency of four. Lurch gave a grey smile and said, we're stronger than the sun. I'd always thought of people who had the capacity to stand alone as being strong. Suddenly, remembering Paul's furry blue letter, his waving arm urging me on, I saw that it could be that apartness was the weak thing.

*

I never look at work emails on the weekend. Paul's answer was waiting for me on Monday morning. He'd sent it in the small hours of Saturday. It was busy that Monday. I didn't get to it till the lunch break.

> *Dear Rob,*
> *Congratulations on your daughter's wedding. That must be satisfying for you. I'm hoping to see our two boys married off one day but it looks unlikely. And to be honest I don't think I'll get "home" anytime soon. My wife's family are on the right. I see another side of things from over here. I don't honestly know if I'll get the chance to call in to see you either, but we'll see.*
> *Cheers,*
> *Paul*

I scrolled down to the email I'd sent him and reread it, uneasily. It was long. Much longer than his answer. The words that I'd thought were unsentimental, avoiding emptinesses, collusive, looked hectoring, a small tirade. I thought of the unknowable paths he'd perhaps thought over to arrive at the few lines of his answer, what he might have edited out. Stuff about what his children did, perhaps, some award he'd won, even. It was hard to imagine any of it. All the sealed in stuff. The mirroring had gone. At last he'd stopped waving.

I clicked the cursor on Reply and the window opened for me to write back. The vertical black line pulsed in the place where I should write. I became aware of the sound of the traffic in the distance. The black line winked about once a second. Some work emails materialised in my inbox while I waited. It was almost the end of the lunch break. After some minutes I closed the window without writing back.

*

A year later I was going back into the office building in the early afternoon. I'd been talking to someone at the lab that morning and knew that some results would be waiting for me in the office. My stomach was heavy with lasagne and I had one of those cartons of coffee with an unnecessarily architectural tight plastic lid.

Roger Bayliss and Chris Johns were standing on the steps talking with arms folded, Chris with an unlit cigarette in her hand. They might have been talking shop so I made to keep walking, but I caught the phrase 'for a drink this weekend' so I slowed.

'Afternoon, colleagues' I said with stock irony. 'Planning future R and D?' The redundancy of 'planning' and 'future' struck me as I said it. But they didn't look as if I'd interrupted anything so I paused on the step.

'Well I am for sure' Chris said. 'The usual Saturday Liquid Research Plan. The SLRP, or *slurp* as I like to call it.' And she took advantage of my cutting in to turn away and light her cigarette.

'Me only maybe' Roger said. Even at rest and with his arms folded he seemed slightly out of breath.

'Not that you can plan the past' I said.

'I was just saying – ' Roger said.

Chris reappeared as it were from behind her own back in a nimbus of smoke.

' – that I rarely get out on a Sunday lunchtime since Paul Fuller died. Used to be my favourite that.'

Chris was doing that thing smokers do of frowning slightly in the fresh smoke and seeming to concentrate, pulling something from her tongue with her fingertips. 'Well I'm going for it' she said. 'It's my fortieth this weekend.'

Roger said, 'Used to drive him to the Wreckers for a sandwich and a pint, not that he was drinking then. Nice view across the Channel. Sometimes his missis drove us so I could have a couple. Most pleasant. Miss that.' He tilted his head back and looked at me through his thick glasses, then forward and over them. 'Thought you knew.'

I shook my head.

'Drank himself to death. Went round the world on his own staying in big hotels on exes. Conferences and meetings in the States, Australia, far east and all that. It was on tap all the time. Some of us can't stand up to it. Praps I'd be the same. There you go. Fucked his liver. They took his leg off last year. That was it.' He started to turn away and as he did so stretched out a hand. For a moment I thought he was offering to shake hands, but he touched my forearm where

I held the lukewarm coffee and moved towards the door. 'Anyway' he said, and gave a small wave as he went.

Chris gave me a look. She moved her eyes upwards in a tiny gesture of exasperation. 'He's just always got somewhere more important to be.'

I cleared my throat. 'I thought you were mates.'

'Hardly. Billy No Mates he is. Or he is now anyway.'

*

In my office I stared at graphs on the screen. The traffic was doing its distant roar. In a building across the street, I could see someone in another office staring at their screen. It lit their face and blanked the glass of their spectacles into metallic mirrors.

Once, I walked beside a river in cold sunlight in the Julian Alps with my wife Amy and my daughter when she was a toddler. The river was shallow and fast over smoothed stones, an unreal, transparent pale green–blue, tinged with minerals leaching out of the rock. The immense wooded valley seemed deserted like a landscape in a dream. There was only the river sound. My daughter, of course, managed to escape from us into the shallow water and splash about briefly, till the cold spoke to her and she stood still, looked hurt, and then cried and I ran in and lifted her out. In memory I take off her shoes and white socks and we dry her perfect white feet with my handkerchief and warm them back to life while she trembles in the cage of my arms.

I didn't look back for Paul's few emails. Perhaps I'd deleted them. Half remembered phrases came to the surface of my mind with new meanings then sank. That last thing, written in the small hours. Cheers.

When we were kids we used to call getting wet through to your sock 'getting a soaker'. With Paul once I'd been walking all day when we got soakers in the river. We were perhaps ten. I often walked on my own all day, around the mountains above the houses, through the pine plantations, tracing ad hoc paths. But this day Paul was with me and it was unusually dry and warm.

I don't know where we'd been. I don't think we'd been aiming to go just to the river. My solitary walks were improvised bound-beatings on secret tracks. No one else was in on some of these. Sometimes the greatest part of the walk was arrival back in the kitchen where you drank off glass after glass of lightfilled, sweet tapwater. The trajectory of these walks was away from and then back to official daily life. So the vague aim, I suppose, was to walk away from people and houses at first. After a while you instinctively avoided others and buildings, and the aura of territory. You become part animal and quick and elusive, like a fox or a badger. The roads people took, like rivers, weren't paths for me but barriers to hurry across.

Anyway, this time with Paul the river was in the way on our return.

And this is the last handkerchief. The river wasn't a pristine miraculous pale green-blue. It was merely clear, and shallow and quick in summer, never more than couple of dozen yards wide, and easy enough to wade across in most places, but we weren't feral enough to wish for a soaker. The valley was the classic glaciated U shape just there. In a few places the river was notched in a veeshaped cut at the bottom of the U, not with erosion but because the banks were built up with waste from iron furnaces in the nineteenth century, and then there were dead, grassed-over coal tips on top of them in places, and sometimes buildings on top of them.

We met the river at the south end of these layers where they began to open into a narrowish band of flood plain. Not that we could read the landscape this way. There was a rubble of gnarled dark rocks along the bank just here which I guess now was slag from demolished furnaces, and scorched sparse yellowish grass growing on it. Mysterious black or rusted pipes stuck out of the water in places, but none of these was near to help our crossing. We looked among the acidic grass for lucky stones. These were intensely black and shiny and sharpedged, probably vitrified pieces of furnace waste. Then we tried to solve the puzzle of how to cross the river. There were lots of limestone rocks sticking dry out of the water. We tried to invent a path across like picking out a constellation. Paul worked one out and tried to point it out to me, gave up, then led the way. Some rocks were firm and some wobbled. Some of the gaps asked for small leaps, and a bet on the solidity of the rock you landed on. As we pantomimed across our feet got wet in increments until Paul yielded one sock up to its destiny and tried to keep the other more or less dry in a strange limp, with one foot in the water and the other on the treacherous stones. The journey must have taken a whole minute.

Quite close to the bank one of us found a paperback wedged against a stone, waving its arms in the water. Though the water looked clean not a lot lived in it. I'd never seen a fish in there. There was often rubbish. A book, though. We dredged it out.

Squelching on the far bank, which was quite flat, we sat down to examine the find. It had a black cover. It wasn't wet right through and if you were careful you could turn the pages. The cover said something about somebody called Molly. *Will Molly take control of her life?*

I peeled open some pages and handed it to Paul. He stared, concentrating, and read, '*She gazed for a moment at his powerful frame. "Perhaps I can help you," she murmured* dem – demmerly, demurely. *She sat back on the hotel-room sofa, softly caressing the trees* –tress? tress – *of hair that hung at the side of her face.* Hair that hung at the side of her face? I don' get it. Anyway. *"Perhaps I can help you," she murmured dem* – murely. *She lay back on the hotel-room sofa, softly caressing the tress of hair that hung at the side of her face. Her voice lowered. "In bed."'* He paused a moment and his eyes lit. 'Hey! This is a dirty book. Wonder if it've got any language in it.'

I'd already leant my head close to his over the book. We peeled back another page. Four or five small tadpoles wriggled on the sodden paper. We lost interest in words and watched them for a while, flexing like escaped commas.

'These haven' got lungs yet' Paul said. 'They need to be in water.' He didn't shut the book but posted it gently back in to river. It drifted, mostly submerged, in a quiet passage of water and swayed against a stone. 'They start eating each other when they grow a bit.'

'I know' I said.

We lay back and looked at the sky. Its curving blueness deepened from pastel at the edges to a moment of profound ultramarine straight over your head. It had a terrifying smoothness. You could fall away into it.

In my office I stared at the spiky steeples and manhattans of the graphs and clicked between them and the grids of figures analysing them. The tiny shapes worked like a sea. I thought of the Atlantic as I've seen it from aeroplanes, by moonlight, quick and trackless with shifting patterns, and the smooth interiors of hotel rooms late at night, the plate glass wall of window a smooth black mirror with the ghost lights of some city, and Paul's ghost afloat over it. Cold light pouring from the open door of the minibar.

The figures and graphs in front of me described the transmutation of one thing into another. They could even let you control it. But I've never understood. I thought of standing in the council house in City Gardens, looking from the smoking hearth to the smoking retort of the blast furnace, of the letters in dark blue on pale blue exhorting me to join something or other. What of any consequence could have happened in the moment that had passed since then?

Paul said, 'Listen.'

The enveloping smoothness of the sky receded a little. I could feel again the hard earth under my back, the dry grass prickling my neck, my sodden socks, heavy and cold around my feet. I listened. I could hear the world again. The river. It wasn't a roar, but a lot of complicated trickling, a lot of threads, a lot of voices laughing, not in one laugh but in the laughter of many conversations. The threads crossed and joined and parted in a dance of so many rhythms and so many tracks that there was none. As I looked at the numbers on the screen, an old man in an armchair, his raincoat belt done up, swam past, and a goldfish made of mirrors with a candleflame tail, and a pigeon that had won a prize and thought it was a medalled general, and pinpricks of light, and orange tadpoles melting into liquid silver, and molten wax, and the imperfect likeness of a quick, intelligent face, glimpsed, so to speak, across a gulf.

HAPTIVOX

1

...during which time he has the most vivid confidence, that he could not have composed less than from two to three hundred lines of poetry; if that indeed can be called composition in which all the images rose up before him as things, with a parallel production of the correspondent expressions, without any sensation of consciousness or effort.

       S.T. Coleridge

The linguistic/physical barrier has been crossed with our new interactive system

       G. Pallander, MD, Haptivox Corp.

After the equipment was installed and they'd taught her how to switch it on, she called him. She said, *Meet me by the fence between the trees and the moor.* They talked.

       *

The fence was straight and went to the horizon. On one side of it there were tall trees and on the other side there was none. A woman came through the trees and stood by the fence, waiting. The sky was overcast and the grass on the treeless side was frosted white like a blank page. At last a man in a dark coat appeared. His body semaphored angular dark shapes as he picked his way. He was out of breath. His face was fresh with the cold and he was quite young. She looked straight into his face and knew every part of it.

She greeted him and suddenly he saw her. Her face was nested in the vee of the upturned collar of her grey coat and the wings of her hair were closed on it. She was unclear against the downstrokes of the trees. Then he could see her eyes and the corner of her mouth smiling, and through a shift of hair the flash of a small earring.

'I like your earrings' he said.

Her hand went up and touched the lobe. 'I didn't know I was wearing them' she said. The hand dropped. 'Come on, you can cross by the stile.'

He saw the stile nearby. It looked black against the whitened ground. He climbed over its A frame and she reached to steady him but they didn't quite touch hands as he stepped down among the trees. His joints were stiff with cold.

'Let me look at you' she said, and she lifted her face close to his and panned her nose close to his upper lip. Her electricity would thaw him.

He stretched his nostrils to smell her but the air was still very cold. It hurt his throat a little, and his eyes.

'You're young' she said.

'Well – '

She pushed a finger against his chest. 'Arguing doesn't work.'

'No. Then so are you.' He touched her face. Some of the numbness melted from his fingers. 'So. Where to?'

'Through the trees. Where else?' She turned from him suddenly, catching his hand and dragging him with her as she walked.

Her coat, he saw, had a fine herringbone pattern. The thin black ribs leant together in rows like indecipherable script.

The blank moorland fell away behind them as they walked and the trees closed in. No branches were so low as to get in their way. Some were lopped so the dark trunks were pothooked and seriffed.

'To my cabin!' She hammed up the words to hide a little embarrassment.

It was as she knew it would be. Dark timber, one door, one window, a chimney.

'Here' she said. She turned to look at him. 'One door, one window, a chimney.'

He looked past her as she spoke and the detail emerged from the quiet gloom. An earring flashed as she turned again and the door was opening. He felt the chill drop from the air as he reached the jamb. He looked at the tongue of hair on her shoulders.

She felt his arms come under hers and his hands close loosely on her breasts. Even through all the layers of clothes she could feel this. He pressed against her back and she turned her head so that his cold mouth brushed her cheek, found the edge of her mouth. She was laughing and he laughed too as they stumbled through the door. He tried to kiss her properly but their teeth collided as she tried to speak.

'Oh, I remember you.'

And they laughed as they tumbled to sit in the threshold and he lay on her and they were still laughing. She put her hand on the back of his neck and tasted his mouth. His lips warmed and filled and she wanted to hug him into the same space as her body, though she didn't say this, and they were struggling to get their clothes out of the way, like that, lying across the threshold, their legs outside on the frosty crunch of dead leaves and her shoulders inside on the floorboards. The lower parts of their coats were parted and she could feel him hard against her as he lay between her legs and frotted at her skirt.

She pushed at the jambs with either hand so that they slid into the room.

'Do you feel how it's warmer?' she said.

'Yes. It's warm on my face and there's a fire in the hearth. Feel it on your face.'

And she could. She turned her head to see the yellow flames. 'Is it coal or wood?'

'Coal?' he said.

'Yes.' And it was. She could see the welded architecture of the black lumps. 'Like when I was a girl.'

'I shut the door' he said, and he shut the door. 'And I take off your shoes. Are they shoes or boots?'

'Oh – ' she stretched out her arms ' – one of each.'

He slid the squaretoed sensible brown shoe off her left foot. Then he unzipped the black boot on her right and slid it the length of her calf and off, held her leg and told her how he kissed it as he kissed it.

'Touch yourself' he said. He whispered it and drew back her skirt and pulled her hand onto her knickers and while her fingertips kneaded there he kissed the length of her leg and then kissed her moving knuckles.

She drew her hand away to open her coat and put her palm on the crown of his head as he sucked at the material until it was wet and he could feel the shape of her through it. She could feel his jaw move as his tongue worked on her. She articulated her hips so that she rolled against his mouth. He looked up along her body and saw her head lying to one side, her eyes shut.

And he sat up and they fumbled at one another's clothes, sliding the zeroes of buttons loose, unhooking clasps and buckles and slipping limbs free of sleeves. She slid his trousers away and saw and felt how ready he was.

The bed was one she could just remember. Her family got rid of it when she was five or six. Highframed and solid, with a footboard, manyblanketed. She drew him to it and sat. It was so high her feet were off the ground. He kissed her and she could taste herself in his mouth. Standing, he slid into her and she lay back and lifted her knees.

He looked at the delta of dark hair, the white page of her skin. She slid back and he climbed onto the bed, a bit awkwardly for all he was so young, but kept inside her, and felt her clench and loosen on him with the pulsing of his hips. He turned her so that he could press his feet against the board.

She felt the thicket of his young hair against her face, pressed her hands against his working back, wrapped her calves at the back of his knees and felt herself open completely. As her eyes rolled up she saw the windowpanes still hieroglyphed with frost.

A little later he said, 'Let's have some wine.' There was a bottle and two glasses on a table by the bed. He laughed. 'We'll leave the tea and jigsaws till much later. Red or white?'

'Red.'

He poured her a glass and she tasted it and it was warm as blood.

'I'll have white' he said, and he poured it from the same bottle.

He kissed her and she could taste the crispness of it against the softness of the red. He dipped his fingertips into his glass and sprinkled droplets on her nipples so that they rose and then he tongued them clean. They put their glasses down and she let him touch her while he kissed her breasts. She knelt on the bed and took some droplets of red and unpacking his head she scattered some wine there and closed her mouth over it. She smiled up at him and moved away, held him as if he were a microphone.

'Hello?' she said. 'Am I receiving you? Come in.'

She laughed and climbed onto him and watched their pubic hair meet and part as he slid into her and away and felt her breasts and hair hang against him. He turned her over and lay on her and he was tight inside her. She started to lose her sense of where she ended and he began, or the bed, or the cabin. The hieroglyphs on the windowpane had melted and streaked into exclamation marks.

'!' they said. '!!. !!!. !!!!'

2

The fact that there is no single-participant version gets rid of the nerd-factor. The system is purely collaborative. Disagreements are literally impossible.

G. Pallander, MD, Haptivox Corp.

Energy is eternal delight

William Blake

In the morning they put him in a chair by the window. He was dry and comfortable and still able to speak. When he had managed to operate the earpiece, he called her. He said, *Wake up, darling. Let's go to the sea.* They talked.

*

She felt him naked and wrapped to the curve of her back so that they made a double-ess. Under the heavy blankets he slid a hand around her hip and found her clitoris.

'Wake up, darling' he said.

She could feel him hardening against her buttocks and wanted to be full with him.

'Come in' she said, and she helped him and they lay cupped together on their sides. His fingertips on her at the front rubbed against him where he entered her.

The cabin was flooded with sunlight. It lit the ceiling as if it were reflected off mirrors, or water. He looked at how it described her shoulder and the long dune of her back.

'Tell me what's outside' he said.

She eased away from him and stood at the window. The frost was gone and the trees were rippling with leaves. There was birdsong.

'I think it's late spring' she said.

'So do I.' He watched her as she leant against the sill and the spring light told him how she looked.

As he spoke she saw the sunlit clearings pulse a more intense green. On the pothook of a sawn branch a swallow hung like a comma.

He was out of bed and pressing lightly against her back. She rubbed her shoulders against his chest and turned to nuzzle his cheek.

'Well, I'm not cold any more' he said.

She arched her back and leant forward and he crouched

a little and entered her again. He watched as he closed on her and ran a hand up the knuckles of her back. It was veiled with fresh sweat and her hair clung to it.

'Too warm in fact.'

She moved from him and turned and pressed to him. They saw that the grate was empty and clean.

'Let's go to the sea' he said.

They opened the door and stepped out and after walking a few yards through the trees were among the dunes.

He remembered the beach at the end of the headland. It clamped a disc of ocean in a sweeping C-shape. At the northern end were the mud cliffs and to the south the rocks where the snorkelling was good. He'd swum there years and years ago. The eastward sea beyond the bay was an immensity of liquefied light. The sun and the moon hung close together in the sky.

As they stood at the edge of this she pressed to him and saw how their shadows overlapped on the hatchwork of coarse grass. Again she wanted to press their bodies through one another into the same space, as she had on the threshold of the cabin, but she couldn't say this. Not quite.

'Today' she said instead, 'today, I want to be you. Just for today.'

He paused and looked at her and said, 'Yes. Then I do too. Come on.'

As they ran across a little stream and down onto the beach she felt her shoulders thicken and her muscles grow heavier.

The water was tepid round her feet after the hot sand. She looked at her new broad feet, felt the heavy purse of her testicles. She saw that he was running his hands over his new hips and breasts.

He looked up at her and laughed. His eyesight was stronger. The sea glittered in tiny sharp points. Her face was long and masculine. He touched it. She was tall. He pressed against her and heard her breathing. He wanted her inside him but couldn't say it yet.

They walked out into the sea and swam. His shorter legs were better for kicking, and he floated so well. He watched her dive among turtles and shoals of neon fish around the southern rocks. They flew over the strange landscape until the seabed fell away and there was nothing but depth under them, and then they let the rhythmic swell carry them back and northward to the mud cliffs.

They stood in the shallows there and he showed her what he'd done as a boy.

'Here' he said. He took a handful of the mud and smeared it on her chest, knelt and worked it round her penis and thighs. 'This keeps the sun off.'

'Is *that* what it's for?' she said, and she took some of it and soothed it over his breasts, wrote her initials on his belly. She held him to her and palmed it across his buttocks. She felt herself harden against him, felt the weight and the tightening of it. She worked the muscle that moved it a little, as she'd felt men do to her.

He knew he was wet. He led her to the edge of the water and pulled her down onto the sand. He dug to make a hollow for his hips and opening himself drew her onto him. She felt the skin pull back along the shaft as she went in, and the way he clenched her. She dug her feet down into the sand and pushed.

'It's very clever how you do that' she said.

'You too' he said. 'I don't know which of us is which.' He put his hands on her buttocks as she tightened and relaxed.

She spread her arms across the sand so that their overlapping bodies made an ex and over her shoulder he watched the wheel of the sky. The colour deepened and the stars came out. With his new eyes he saw them sharper than childhood. Cassiopeia swung above the mud cliffs first as a double-you and then, as it revolved around the Pole Star, an em.

'Why don't we get tired?' he said.

The stars flared and faded in time with their movement. Then the light held its intensity and he braced himself against her. The lights strengthened and grew, swelling and joining so that the whole sky whitened blank as a sheet. He held his breath.

She felt how close he was and thought that she would burst inside him. Her toes clenched in the sand.

The whiteness spread until the cliffs and the headland and the rocks and the sea and they themselves were annihilated by it. Then she burst and emptied into him. The world refilled with colours, and the filmy thread of the Milky Way and an alphabet of constellations threw themselves across the sky.

Her weight slackened on him and she laughed. She moved away and touched him for a long time because she knew that he would be slower in coming down.

The sky over the sea was turning pale. Lying next to her, he touched his breast and ran the other hand through his pubic hair to rest a finger lightly on his clitoris and between his lips. As the sun was about to rise he felt the breast withering and hardening into muscle, the nipple retracting. The arm across his abdomen got heavier, the pudendum under his fingers swelling back into a penis and testicles. He felt his legs lengthening and coarse hair growing on them. While this happened he watched her breasts and hips swell, her flesh soften and her hair thicken. She put a hand to his face and stroked it.

He shivered. 'Somebody's treading on my grave' he said. 'I think we should go back.'

And though the sun was coming up, the air had chilled a little.

3

This is more than a plaything. As it has no harmful effects, and participants need only be lucid, able to think and speak, even if only in a murmur, it can have many beneficial functions. Gerontologists are currently trialling its potential in palliative care.

G. Pallander, MD, Haptivox Corp.

Language is the incarnation of thought.

Wordsworth

As soon as the assistants left her alone she pushed the jigsaw and her cup aside. She didn't like them to hear her muttering. She switched on the earpiece and called him. He was asleep at first, but eventually he woke and answered. After a while he remembered who she was. He was slurring a little, but she could understand him. *Let's walk*, she said. *Meet me in the trees.* They talked.

*

She was leaning against a tree, waiting. He had walked down off the autumn-yellowed mountain into her forest and he was still a little numb. She smiled.

'Hello, you' she said.

She was wearing a dark coat, its front open, and under it a yellow frock patterned with a fine black print. Pale patches of sunlight washed across her.

'I like that yellow frock' he said. He was a little out of breath. 'I haven't seen you wear it in years.'

She looked down at herself. 'I didn't even realise I'd put this one on' she said.

He kissed her. Her breathing was shallow and a little anxious.

'Are you all right?' she said.

'Yes. It's not so cold down here. Are you?'

'I'm always nervous at first when we meet. Let's walk.'

He put his arm round her as they went. He could smell her hair, her skin. 'It's a funny thing' he said. 'I felt half dead up there, but, god, talking to you brings me to life.' He felt his limbs loosen.

'Do you remember this place?' she said.

They'd come to a stream. He stepped onto a large stone in the middle of it and pulled her on after him. They stood front to front in the middle of the stream.

'Yes' he said. He slid his arms under her coat, round her back and downwards over the flare of her buttocks. He thought of her, firm and packed away and waiting for him. 'Alph. The sacred river. L'origine du monde.'

'Show-off' she said. She squeezed herself to his dark jacket. She wanted their trunks to fuse.

He stepped to the other bank and she followed.

Nearby was a place among the trees full of dried dead leaves. Their chiselled shapes were effs and ees and curly jays. She pulled him down among them. His hand under her dress was cold, but it didn't matter.

'We lay here together once' he said. 'Years ago when we were young.'

'Yes.' She undid his trousers and brought him to life. She straddled him with her face towards his feet and sucked him and rubbed herself against his face. He gathered her skirts away and pulled aside her pants so that he could tongue her and they rolled onto their sides and made an endless loop.

'I want to be in you' he said.

She slid her knickers off and sat astride him. 'Let me do it' she said, and she worked on him with her dress spread across his lap.

He could feel her lips kneading round his thickness. 'Yes, I remember' he said. 'It's the same dress. I remember it.'

She watched his face and touched herself where he went in. His hands were on her hips, tightening and relaxing in time with her. She smiled but he didn't smile back.

Above her the sky had clouded. He felt cold where she ground him against the leaves. Tiny flecks of ice were falling on him. He tried to sit up, to pull her trunk to his. They rolled onto their sides and hugged.

She felt him shivering a little. She was wound around him and he was still inside her. She held him tighter.

'We can go back into the cabin' she said. 'It's just here.'

He looked, and the door was a few yards away. They got up and moved to the threshold. The door was stiff. He hugged her again.

'Do you know' she said, 'do you know what I want sometimes when I'm holding you like this?'

He smiled. The door had opened a little and they were standing in the jamb, but the flecks of snow were blowing on his jacket. He rubbed his lips against the fine print on her yellow collar. 'Oh, I can read you like a book.'

She said, 'I want to occupy the same space as you.'

'Yes' he said. 'I've felt that too. Yes.'

They lay down on the threshold of the cabin and she squeezed against him. Their brows, noses, chins, slid through one another. He felt his torso ease through hers. It seemed to her that they were like two huge buildings, or cities, with their complications of floors and passageways, stairwells and liftshafts, the lacework of girders and fills of brick and concrete and then the surges of electricity and fluids, the traffic and commerce of every day. Imagine all that thinning and becoming porous, and then these two universes interpenetrating, the stairwells from different buildings intertwining and joining, the skeletal architectures permeating one another and interlocking. The mechanical inhabitings of sex, the crude transformations on the beach were nothing to this, where the different-same energies whispered in the different-same channels. And he felt this too. All the space that matter is made of suddenly understood itself, and was generous, and let the other in. Their different grammars and lexicons didn't just blend into a creole. They atomized as they crossed and reconfigured. And once this had happened there could be no images, nothing to observe, only this new building, with nothing outside its own self-awareness and an apprehension of the marvellous.

And immediately some part of this new place started to fail. Images started to return of lights going out and pipework cooling, a sense of some shrivelled, hard thing disconnecting itself back into being.

She lay against him on the threshold. He didn't move. The snow fell in tiny pieces on his dark jacket. Eventually it would white him out. But for now it was a scattering, and it wasn't true, what they said about the flakes. They weren't all unique. Each was a word and they were identical.

'Yes' they said. 'Yes. Yes.'

OPENING TIME

I felt my flesh assembling on the bars, plates and scoops of bone. The muscles bunched into balls at the bases of my thumbs. Flaps of skin furled themselves on my shins. The jelly of my eyes came into being and fashioned itself into bulbs. There was a small, twitching sensation in my skull as the nerves knitted themselves between reshaping brain and retina.

I have only a fleeting and uncertain recollection of this as the brain and other soft stuff, having rotted first, came fully back into being last.

There was no sudden quiver of life or anything dramatic like that. I was aware of my weight flattening my buttocks, my feet hanging to one side, twisting the relinked columns of bone, muscle, sinew and ligament in my legs. A mild popping passed through me with the reopening of arteries and veins. My jaw pulled up against its own weight, set the rows of teeth into their old bite.

My teeth.

The new tongue moved easily along the rows feeling them carefully and in my mind I made a picture of them. Real teeth, the gums overlapping them firm and unreceded.

The earth around my face was not pressing hard, had merely leaked through rotting patches in the lid, perhaps. Or no, there must have been endless ages and all that would be gone. Still it felt very loose.

I rolled my head slightly to one side, tried gingerly to raise a hand. There was no strain, no stiffness. I felt that the soil was gently gathering itself away from me. It parted to left and right from the centre of my chest. My face, I thought, was clear. Opening my eyes I glimpsed some fragments of mud pulling away from my eyelids. I got to my feet without feeling any effort.

All around me people were getting up out of the earth. In some places dozens rose out of a single space one behind the other, sometimes in pairs. The effect was comic and for a moment I laughed and saw that others were laughing too. That passed. The ground was pocked with shallow craters of loose earth endlessly disturbed by the rising people. Some lay staring at the sky, which was not blinding but veiled with thin, pale grey cloud. Others jumped up and ran. Some, Like me, got up carefully and looked around. They mostly looked about twenty-five, though some looked younger. There were children too, and quite a lot of babies, some of them very tiny and bald. They, quicker than anyone, stood and ran, looking very happy, even the ones that scarcely looked old enough to have been born.

I looked at my hands and felt my face and hair. There were no wallets of withered skin on my wrists and neck. I had lips that curved out and were fleshy. The hair was thick over my skull. There were no liverish splotches on the back of my hands. My knuckles were not swollen. My fingers flexed without clicking. My wedding ring was gone.

I looked down into my crater, from which more people were coming. My wife had not emerged with me. I recognised none of the people around me. We were all dressed the same, in clean and comfortably fitted suits made, somehow, of one piece of material which seemed to have no fastenings. The cloth was a pale pastel colour which I cannot put a name to.

Still looking at my finger ends I began to walk with the others. Running, walking or stumbling, we all went in the same direction and although people sprang out of the earth everywhere the crowd was spread so that you could walk without being pressed faster than you wanted to go.

After walking a long time I came to two tall brick pillars which gave the impression of a gate. As I passed between them among many others I looked back and saw, into the endless distance, the broken ground with young people and children still rising. When I went outside – it seemed as if beyond the pillars was outside – I saw that I was on a large plain of cinders. At a little distance it was neutral and colourless but underfoot it hinted at a dull, long-cooled red under the surface.

All around, as far as I could see, people ran or walked, still in the one direction. It might have been a trick of the perspective, but when I looked in that direction the crowd seemed to converge and the air above that horizon was tinged with a smirched orange pall.

I walked too, and tried to keep pace with a tall young woman with dark hair.

'Excuse me' I said. She did not look round though I thought she had heard me. 'Excuse me, but could you – ' I realised that I did not know what I wanted to ask.

She glanced at me and said something in a language I could not identify.

I stopped and she went on, not glancing back.

I looked around me at the people streaming past. What were the chances of finding someone who spoke my language? I noticed that a few people, like me, were standing still like fenceposts in a flooded river. Then I saw one young man walking in a different direction. Apart from that he was unremarkable, dressed as were the rest of us. I looked more carefully and saw another, a woman, I thought, walking against the crowd. I walked sideways, so to speak, for a couple of dozen paces. It was not difficult. The walkers were still well spread. From my new position I saw a few others walking away or across the flow. I noticed that the children never walked anywhere but in the orthodox direction, and mostly more quickly than the others.

I turned and walked back through the crowd. If I had continued, I thought, the people would begin to bunch and I would be wedged, unable to turn.

Facing this way, I had the sensation that I was looking downhill, though I could see that I was still on the cinder plain. It was curious to look into the oncoming faces, some preoccupied, others smiling and without cares. For the most part they took no notice of me. One man paused and spoke words I did not understand, nodding to the place at my back, and then went on. Walking away was very easy and the feeling of travelling downward, despite the evidence of my eyes, persisted.

After a long time the crowd thinned further. The milky grey veil across the sky grew brighter. Somehow, so gradually that I did not notice it happening, my picture of walking on a plain and my sensation of descending adjusted to one another and I was walking down an undulating slope of cinders and shale. There were very few walkers passing me at this point and when the slope suddenly dropped steeply before me, I realised there were none.

I half slid down the crumbling reddish shale and onto tussocky mountainside which continued downhill before me. Overhead the thin cloud was shredding like ripe cloth, revealing the blue.

I knew the place well. I walked down the mountain over the rushes and coarse grass onto a rough track, down to the familiar council estate on a lip of hill a few hundred feet above the valley bed. It was a sunny day in spring and it had rained recently so that the air was scrubbed and all the colours were sharp. Even the drab red brick of the council houses and their metal window frames were precise and pleasing in the sharp light. Across the valley, the other hill, ribbed with terraces lower down and patched with fir plantations and moorland above, was darkened sometimes by the dragged shadow of a cloud. I plucked a grass as I walked down to the estate.

In the top street were the usual dogs, the bus parked at the end of its route for a few minutes. I walked through a gap between the gardens and the next street, down past the rusting garages of corrugated metal and around the corner. I stopped at the fourth, familiar gate.

Under my shoes of nameless pastel, pale brown earth clung between the tarmac chippings. The paint on the corner of the steel gate was flaked in the remembered way. I lifted the chain and went in.

The back door was open. On the back step, a white and tan cat, half grown, was sunning himself, licking a wrist with his claws flicked out. A film of milk was drying in a saucer nearby, which sat on the place where the ashes from the fire were tipped. At the end of the garden a woman stood, talking to a neighbour across the fence, which was of wire strung on concrete posts. She rested one hand on the fencepost as she talked, and one foot rested on its toe. It reminded me of the way ponies sometimes stand with one hoof resting lightly on its front edge.

I went into the house. In the frying pan on the cooker were sizzling discs of black pudding. The gas was low so they'd do slowly. With mild surprise I recognised the pattern printed on the kitchen oilcloth.

I walked into where I knew the livingroom would be. There was a newish fire in the grate, the lumps of coal vaulting a burning orange space. On the mantelpiece was the buff coloured, square faced clock, the salt and pepper pots. A boy aged about ten lay on the floor reading a comic, absorbed.

There came the smell of carbolic soap, the sound of breathing, slightly laboured. A man, youngish, had come into the kitchen and, glancing into the frying pan as he passed, unbuckled the belt of his raincoat. He came into the livingroom, not looking at me, and put an Oxo tin which he had carried under one arm onto the table. The boy and he exchanged greetings. The man, as I knew he would, put a hand into his pocket and brought out a tube of sugared sweets. The boy took them saying thanks and went on reading, peeling back the silver paper of the tube. The man stood watching for a moment as the boy put the first sweet in his mouth and champed at it.

I looked out of the window. People passed, and on the far mountain a bus moved. All these people, I thought, except one, were walking towards an orange smirch in a milky grey sky, and I would have to go back up the hill and over the shale and across the cinders with them. I thought of the gritty chippings of sugar lodging between the boy's teeth and I knew that whatever lay at the end of my walk, it could not be paradise.

ABOUT THE AUTHOR

Christopher Meredith is the author of four novels and various collections of poetry in English and a book for children in both Welsh and English. He also translates Welsh fiction and poetry into English. He was born and brought up in Tredegar and lives in Brecon.

Shifts

by Christopher Meredith

Pb £8.99
ISBN: 185411199X

Jack Priday returns to his hometown at the end of the 1970s after nine years' absence. His life becomes entangled with those of old friends Keith, Judith and O while the heavy industry that defined and moulded the town crumbles. *Shifts* is a profound examination of the relationship between our inner lives, the people around us, the forces of history, and the possibilities of grasping or controlling these.

'Like very great novels, the power of *Shifts* is to evoke universal themes in a believably rendered microcosmic reality. ... if... we seek to venerate a book that helps us understand ourselves and our circumstances, and that uses the novel's power to investigate the psychological fallout of socio-historical trauma while at the same time being skip-along readable and viciously funny, let's stop the search here.' Dylan Moore in *Wales Arts Review*, nominating *Shifts* as his choice for the Greatest Welsh novel of All Time.

'A beautiful, understated first novel' *New York Times Review of Books*

'A first novel of consummate skill' *Sunday Times*

Griffri

by Christopher Meredith

Pb £5.95
ISBN: 1854111302

On two nights separated by a gap of a dozen years, Griffri ap Berddig, a poet at the court of a minor Welsh prince of the twelfth century, tells his life story to a Cistercian monk. Part boast and part confession, his words turn into a compelling narrative which develops through an accumulation of obsessive images towards self-revelation. A complex mixture of historical detail and invention, *Griffri* is a serious and entertaining novel examining the limits of our knowledge of the world and ourselves.

'This extraordinary novel takes historical fiction and runs with it as far as it can go' *The Historical Novel Society's Review*

'A book of uncommon interest and appeal' *The Guardian*

Sidereal Time

by Christopher Meredith

Pb £7.95
ISBN: 1854112392

Clint and Dustin are coconuts, 10L have turned into three-toed sloths, Gron is becoming Zero Mostel, the lower sixth is an airliner of people about to fall out of the sky, and you, you've turned into a three-eyed Martian who speaks a nounless language and has forgotten to pay the child minder. But what's all this got to do with sixteenth century Ermland?

It's an ordinary week in post-industrial south Wales, and alienated desperation is as much fun as it's ever been. Sidereal Time, starting with the experiences of Sarah, a school teacher feeling the first intimations of middle age, explores the cussed paradox of the way life can be predictable and yet not follow any script you've prepared.

'An amazingly brave, funny and touching book' *Time Out*

'Inspired' *The Guardian*

The Book of Idiots

by Christopher Meredith

Pb £8.99
ISBN: 9781854115652

Tipsy, sick Wil Daniel tells the narrator, Dean, a tale that may be a ghost story or a romance, a farce or a tragedy. Meanwhile we get glimpses of Dean's own half-lived life, and those of friends and colleagues. Can Clive regain the triumphs he achieved at the age of nine? Will Jeff stop his swimming trunks from dissolving? These threads develop into a dark, offbeat and merciless examination of maleness and mortality.

Outstanding in its use of dialogue to reveal character, this superbly written novel develops into a meditation on kinds of suffering that are no less acute for being routine.

'A literary masterpiece' *Western Mail*

'A darkly comic triumph full of uncomfortable truths' *Short-List Magazine*